Benjamin Lovell might pretend modesty in his perfect plain suit. But the man was a trumped-up peacock, near to choking on his own pride.

He'd decided, without even meeting her, that he would have dear, sweet, innocent Belle—just to gain a seat in the House of Commons.

Something must be done, and it must be done immediately.

Amy stood suddenly, almost bumping into a young man balancing far too many glasses of lemonade.

Suddenly she had a plan.

She responded with a simpering laugh. 'La, sir. It is a relief to see you. I retired to the corner for I was parched and near to fainting.'

She reached out and took two of his lemonades, taking a sip from the first. 'Much better,' she said, giggling again and ignoring his astonishment at her rudeness.

Then, as if she was as unsteady as she claimed, she turned and staggered forward the two steps necessary to stand before Benjamin Lovell. She wavered, lurched, and allowed herself a brief, triumphant smile. Then she dumped the contents of the glasses in her hand down his elegant white waistcoat.

Author Note

This book gave me an excuse to use one of my favourite bits of Regency research. In the days before the advent of telephone and telegraph, written communication was the only way to stay in touch, and *everyone* was a master of correspondence. They found methods beyond word-choice to get a big message into a small space.

Since the recipients were the ones to pay postage on their mail, it was rude to make them pay for a long and heavy letter. To this end, there were no envelopes. The paper the letter was written on was folded and sealed with wax, and addressed on the blank side.

To cheat a second page into a one-page letter writers turned the paper ninety degrees and wrote the second half over the top of the previously written first page. It was up to the reader patiently to decipher the crossed words.

It made a sharp pen nib and good handwriting all the more important. I think of my own unreadable penmanship and stand in awe.

THE WEDDING GAME

Christine Merrill

This is a work of fiction. Names, characters, places, locations and incidents are purely fictional and bear no relationship to any real life individuals, living or dead, or to any actual places, business establishments, locations, events or incidents. Any resemblance is entirely coincidental.

First published in Great Britain 2[illegible]
By Mills & Boon, an imprint of HarperCollins*Publishers*
1 London Bridge Street, London, SE1 9GF

Large Print edition 2017

ISBN: 978-0-263-06763-7

Our policy is to use papers that are natural, renewable and recyclable products and made from wood grown in sustainable forests. The logging and manufacturing processes conform to the legal environmental regulations of the country of origin.

Printed and bound in Great Britain
by CPI Antony Rowe, Chippenham, Wiltshire

Christine Merrill lives on a farm in Wisconsin, USA, with her husband, two sons, and too many pets—all of whom would like her to get off of the computer so they can check their e-mail. She has worked by turns in theatre costuming and as a librarian. Writing historical romance combines her love of good stories and fancy dress with her ability to stare out of the window and make stuff up.

Books by Christine Merrill

Mills & Boon Historical Romance

The de Bryun Sisters

The Truth About Lady Felkirk
A Ring from a Marquess

Ladies in Disgrace

Lady Folbroke's Delicious Deception
Lady Drusilla's Road to Ruin
Lady Priscilla's Shameful Secret

Stand-Alone Novels

A Wicked Liaison
Miss Winthorpe's Elopement
Dangerous Lord, Innocent Governess
Two Wrongs Make a Marriage
Unlaced at Christmas
'The Christmas Duchess'
The Secrets of Wiscombe Chase
The Wedding Game

Mills & Boon Historical *Undone!* eBooks

Seducing a Stranger
Virgin Unwrapped
To Undo a Lady

Visit the Author Profile page at millsandboon.co.uk for more titles.

To 2017.
You are still bright and unspoiled.

Please be more gentle and loving to us all than last year was.

Chapter One

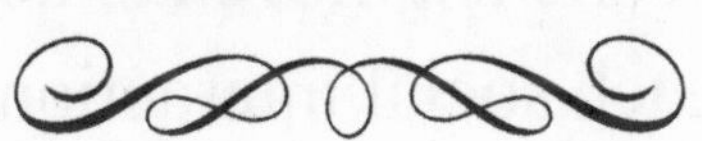

As they always were at the height of the London Season, Almack's Assembly Rooms were crowded to the point of overflowing. Amelia Summoner circled the edges of the main room, watching the marriage-minded throng unobserved. It was easy to do when one knew the place and people in it as well as she did.

She had not missed a Wednesday in the three years her family had had vouchers. In that time she had watched three crops of debutantes arrive, parade and depart on the arms of the gentlemen who married them. She had made her own come-out the first year and, after a brief splash, she had sunk through the waters of society, forgotten.

Now she moved about the place like a fish in

the deep, invisible until the moment she chose to be otherwise. Unlike other unattached girls of her age, she viewed this more as a freedom than a failure. It was more relaxing to dance, speak or flirt only when one felt moved to do so, instead of obsessing on each social interaction as if it was to be a life-changing event. If one simply wished to watch others, it was much better to be *that Summoner girl.*

No. Not the pretty one. The other one. The odd one.

After her first few balls, she had known that she was not going to be a major success. She had been classified by the patronesses as an 'unconventional beauty with an excessively sharp wit'. Any other girl would have been hurt by such a damning compliment. It did not take a bit of Amy's vaunted intelligence to know that only her desirable family name kept her from being labelled 'plain and opinionated'. A connection by marriage to Lord Summoner could make a young man's future, in politics or society. But even those men were hoping for a wife who was conventional in all ways and excessively pretty, rather than excessively sharp.

But it was Amy's intention to remain just as she was. Thus far, her character had been formed without compromise and she was satisfied with the result. She'd yet to meet a man for whom she was willing to change. In the face of her stubborn refusal to aid in their ambitions by marrying them, even the most stalwart of suitors had given up wooing her ages ago. This Season, if a gentleman wished to dance with her, she knew it was out of pity.

More likely, it was because he wanted to be seen as the nice sort of fellow who bestowed his friendship evenly about the family, and was willing to stand up with her quiz of an older sister if it would make Miss Belle Summoner smile. This year, London buzzed with talk of Lord Summoner's younger daughter, the most celebrated beauty of the decade. Tonight, as she moved through the crowd, Amy had overheard more than a few men sighing that a single smile from that delicate beauty, Belle, would be worth any sacrifice up to and including being nice to Miss Amelia, the spinster.

No one had dared to try it yet and Amy had no intention of being an easy target for their cheap flattery. She moved through the crush with a purposeful step that hinted a destination in mind and no time for interruption. When she sat, it was in a corner, with her fan raised, scanning the crowd as if looking for someone other than the people in the immediate vicinity. She kept her acquaintance limited, knowing that people would not dare to speak to her without an introduction. If she did not deign to know them, then they could not use her as a conduit to meet Belle.

Since she did not have to waste her time on dancing and idle chatter, she could watch and listen. She heard dozens of conversations without being a part of any of them, while scanning the opposite side of the room to catch those that watched her sister with more than casual interest. If a gentleman in tonight's crowd was seriously interested in Belle, Amy would know his intentions almost before he did himself. Then she could prepare the proper defence against him. It would take a very special man to make a match with Arabella. No others need apply.

Tonight alone, Amy had catalogued and discounted a dozen prospective suitors. Their intentions did not matter if they lacked sufficient money, manners or station to get around Father's plans for his daughters. He expected them to marry well, if they married at all. After years of trying to find a husband for Amy, Lord Summoner had declared her too headstrong to wed a man who was not of her own choosing and agreed to let her be.

But Belle…

Amy hid a sigh behind her fan. Belle would be very easily led, by Father or anyone else. It was good that she had a sister to look out for her and keep her from harm.

And it was not as if she did not want Belle to marry and be happy. Though there were many ne'er-do-wells and fortune hunters in London, there were some promising candidates as well. As Amy found them, she scrawled their names on the back of her empty dance card for further investigation. So far, there were fully eight men who might make a good match for Belle. They were neither too young nor too old, at least passably handsome, good tempered, well born and rich, but not high flyers. A union with any of them might result in pleasant rustication for most of the year and not too much strenuous socialising.

After separating sheep from goats in tonight's field, there was but one man who fit neither category. He was the one Amy found the most worrisome. As she watched Benjamin Lovell, she did not need to hear his words to know that he was shopping for a wife.

Though Mr Lovell might pretend that he had come to London's most popular marriage mart for a few dances and a light supper, he made too great a show of uninterest to be completely sincere. He stood at the side of the room, feigning boredom to the point of turning his back to the dance floor. But he had positioned himself so that he might gaze in one of the mirrors on the wall to watch and catalogue the females in the room just as carefully as she had been watching the males.

False apathy often proved more dangerous to the hearts and minds of young ladies than active pursuit. In response to his neglect, the gentle sex worked all the harder to get his attention. It was what he sought from them, she was sure. He wished to be the prey, rather than the hunter. It was a bold strategy for a man of uncertain parentage and she admired him for it.

Apparently, the patronesses admired him as well. No amount of money was sufficient to sway them into giving vouchers to a gentleman who was not worthy to marry into the finest families in England. Illegitimacy was a stain that not all men could rise above. But rumour had it that Mr Lovell was the most exclusive sort of bastard.

His Grace the Duke of Cottsmoor had not made a formal acknowledgement of Mr Lovell, but it must have been intended. Before Cottsmoor's sudden death, Mr Lovell had often been seen in the company of the Duke and his Duchess. They had treated him as family even though they said nothing about his origins. When the Duke, the Duchess and their first born had all been taken by an influenza, Mr Lovell had withdrawn from society for a year, mourning them as lost parents and brother.

His birth and early life were shrouded in secrecy. He had been educated abroad, which raised a few eyebrows from those graduates of Oxford or Cambridge with the most school loyalty. But one could hardly blame Cottsmoor for not sending his bastard to the same school as his heir.

Mr Lovell had lost nothing by his Continental learning. His speech was flawless and no gaps had been found in his knowledge. He was thought intelligent without being didactic, witty without conceit and capable of wise counsel, but able to hold his tongue when his opinion was not required. Because of this, the new Cottsmoor, still too young for university, sometimes came to him for advice in navigating his new role as peer.

If the only flaw was that his noble father had not bothered to marry his mother? After meeting the charming Mr Lovell, society had declared it was hardly any fault at all. In fact, it might even be an advantage. The Duke had left a bequest to see that his natural son was amply provided for. According to gossip, Mr Lovell was turning his inheritance into even more money with smart investments.

But one would not have realised it, without careful observation. He did not call attention to his newly acquired wealth in his dress. His tailoring was impeccable, which made him no different than all the other gentlemen in the room. But the choices of fabric, with the richness of the black coat offsetting a white vest of expensive silk brocade, whispered that he was fashionable, but no dandy.

The buckles on his knee breeches were not overly large or brassy. But when one took the time to notice, one noted their heaviness and the dull gleam of silver. He wore no rings or jewellery other than the fob on his watch and that was all but hidden under his coat front. It only peeped into view when he danced, revealing a heavy gold chain that ended in a shockingly large emerald that winked as if to say, *I have money, but the confidence not to flaunt it in public.*

His valet had not bothered with a complicated knot for his cravat. It was done up in an Oriental so simple he might have managed it himself. The blinding white accented the sharp, dark line of his jaw. He had the same colouring as the rest of the Cottsmoor line, distinctive dark eyes and hair, and the faint olive cast to the skin. If the young Duke grew to be half as handsome as Mr Lovell, he would not need a title to send ladies scurrying for his approval.

But tonight, it was Mr Lovell who held the attention, of all the girls in the room. Of course, Amy's fascination was purely academic. She fluttered her fan to cool the sudden heat on her face. She was not doting on the man. She merely needed to assure herself that he was no threat to Belle. If Mr Lovell was unworthy, it did not matter what Lady Jersey thought of him. He would not get so much as an introduction.

But if he was as good as he seemed?

She fanned herself again. If he was capable of being a kind and loving husband who gave as much attention to his wife as he did to his carefully crafted persona, then Amy could not hope for a better match for her sister.

She drifted in his direction, pretending to admire the line of dancers on the floor. Watching such a handsome man should have been pleasing, but there was something about this one that left her uneasy. Benjamin Lovell was too good to be true. Amy could not shake the feeling that his artless perfection was calculated more precisely than the fine watch on the other end of the emerald fob.

A part of her could not blame him. Who amongst them did not wear a mask from time to time? But it would have made more sense, were he poor. If his money was real, as it obviously was, he had no reason to be disingenuous.

With a flutter of her fan she moved closer, then past them to a chair in the corner where the candlelight from the chandeliers could not quite reach. It afforded her an excellent position to see both Mr Lovell and his friend Mr Guy Templeton in quarter-profile as they chatted.

Though the movement was almost imperceptible, Mr Templeton was shifting from foot to foot. Then, with a quick glance to check for observers that missed Amy entirely, he reached down to give his knee breeches a yank on each leg, and shifted again. 'Damn things keep riding up,' he muttered to Mr Lovell. 'It gives a new meaning to Almack's balls.'

The polite smile on Mr Lovell's face barely wavered. 'They are the price of gentility, Templeton. No lady of quality will have you if you cannot stand patiently in formal wear.'

'They are nothing more than a nuisance,' he insisted. 'I wonder, is it necessary to examine our legs before making their purchase, as if we are horseflesh?'

'Legs and wind,' Lovell agreed, with a casual gesture toward the dance floor. 'You had best prove to them you can gallop. With pins like those holding you up, you will not get a woman to take you unless you pad your calves. At the very least, we must get you a better tailor. You wear that suit like it is full of fleas.'

'Because it itches,' Templeton agreed. Then he sighed happily. 'But the girl I've got my eye on will have me even so.'

'She will need to be the most patient creature in London to put up with you,' Lovell said, 'if you will not attend to the niceties.'

Not too patient, thought Amy. With a good family, a pleasant face and a full purse, Mr Templeton was near the top of her list for prospective brothers-in-law.

'Niceties be damned,' said Templeton under his breath, offering a polite nod to a passing patroness. 'Old bats like that one insist on breeches, call tea and cake a supper, and do not allow so much as a waltz with a pretty girl. Then they make the introductions, thinking they can decide our marriages for us. Worse yet, they make us pay for the privilege.'

'It seems to work well enough,' Lovell said with a shrug.

'But if we truly love, can we not choose a more direct method to demonstrate our feelings? It is like standing on a river bank,' Templeton said, gesturing at a group of girls on the opposite side of the room. 'But instead of simply swimming across to the object of our desire, we have to pick our way across the water on slippery rocks.'

'Swim?' Lovell arched his eyebrows in mock surprise. 'The water would spoil one's knee breeches. And what makes you think romantic emotion has anything to do with the process of picking a wife?'

The words were delivered in a tone of cold calculation so at odds with the pleasantly approachable expression on Mr Lovell's strikingly handsome face that Amy almost dropped her fan in shock. She regained her grip and fluttered deliberately, staring away from them so they could not see her flush of annoyance. He was a heartless fraud, just as she'd suspected.

'Not love and desire one's future wife?' Templeton said in genuine surprise. 'Is that not half the fun of getting one?'

'Fun.' Lovell's lip twitched in revulsion, as if he had found a fly in his lemonade. 'Marriage is far too serious an undertaking to be diminished by idle pleasure.'

Then the grimace disappeared and the smile returned. But his stance, shoulders squared and one foot slightly forward, was the one her father took when on the verge of political oratory. He used the same distancing posture when encouraging her to conform to society and find a husband who would improve her weak character so her father did not have to.

To the last vertebra of his inflexible British

spine, Mr Lovell was a man who knew how things should be and had no qualms in telling others the truth as he saw it. 'When one marries, one does not just make a match with the young lady, one enters into a union with her family and with society as well.'

'I should think it was unnecessary for you to think of such things,' Templeton pointed out. 'Cottsmoor, after all—'

Lovell cut him off with a raised hand. 'For argument's sake, let us assume that I have no family at all. I am the first of my line, which makes it all the more important that I choose my attachments wisely. Picking the right father-in-law will do more for a man of ambition than choosing the right woman ever will.'

'Then you want a man with a title,' Templeton interrupted. 'The Duke of Islington is rich as Croesus and has three daughters, all of age.'

Lovell shook his head. 'Title is hereditary and lands are entailed. And I do not need his money. I am quite capable of making my own.'

'No title.' Templeton stroked an imaginary beard as if deep in thought. 'You don't need to marry for money. But of course, you will tell me the daughter of a cit is not good enough for you.'

'Nor scholars or men of law,' Lovell agreed. 'I want a proper Tory with an old fortune, distantly related to Pitts, elder and younger. Someone who dines with Wellington and has Grenville's ear.'

Amy leaned forward in alarm.

'Politics?' Templeton said with surprise.

'If one wishes to make a difference in society, where else would one be than Parliament?'

'And you are speaking of Lord Summoner, of course.'

'No other,' Lovell agreed and Amy's heart sank.

'I assume you wish to wed the lovely Arabella?' Templeton said with a bark of a laugh.

'She is the toast of the Season,' Lovell said. 'I mean to settle for nothing less than the best of the best.'

'Then you must get in line behind the rest of the men in London,' Templeton replied, shaking his head. 'Her dance card was nearly full before we even arrived. I had to fight a fellow for the last spot.'

'I did not bother. I have not yet gained an introduction to her,' Lovell said. 'There must be nothing less than respectable in our first meeting.'

Amy's mind raced to stay ahead of him. His insistence on propriety was a small consolation. It meant there was still time to stop him.

'Even when you do manage to meet her, you will find it a challenge to draw her out,' Templeton informed him. 'She is very shy. Her smile is dazzling, but she speaks hardly at all.'

'All the better,' Lovell replied. 'Who would wed a woman like that for conversation?'

The bone handle of Amy's fan snapped beneath the pressure of her fingers. This odious man was speculating over Belle as if she was nothing more than an afterthought in his plans. Even worse, she suspected the comment about a lack of conversation was a reference to something no true gentleman should speak of when referring to a lady.

Apparently, Templeton agreed. 'See here, Lovell…'

Lovell held up his hands in denial. 'I meant no slight to the lady. But one does not have to marry any woman for intellectual stimulation when one's goal is to take a seat amongst the wisest men in English society.'

Amy raised her fan to hide her smirk. Having met some of her father's friends, Mr Lovell had a view of male superiority that was charming in its naivety.

He continued with his plans. 'I want to wed a woman who is beautiful and talented, who will do credit to my home and bear and raise my children.' He thought for a moment. 'And to win the most sought-after girl of the year will reflect well on my taste and on my abilities of persuasion. I want to be the best and I will settle for nothing less than the best from those around me. But as I said before, it is less about winning the girl and more about winning her father. He has control of two seats in the House of Commons and I mean to be in one of them by year's end. If he is here tonight, I will seek him out and find my way into his good graces. Once I have done that, the rest will follow.'

Bastard.

Another spine of her fan snapped, but Amy barely felt it. Bastard was too accurate to be an insult to his character. There were probably a great many epithets she would have used to describe him, were she a man, and Benjamin Lovell deserved every last one. He might pretend modesty in his perfect, plain suit. But the man was a trumped-up peacock, near to choking on his own pride. Without even meeting her, he'd decided he must have dear, sweet, innocent Belle, just to gain a seat in the House of Commons. He would not give a thought to her, once they were married. Worse yet, if he wished for the best from those around him, he might take out his disappointment upon her sister when he realised she was unequal to his ambitious plans.

Something must be done and it must be done immediately. Amy stood, almost bumping into a young man who was working his way along the edge of the room, balancing far too many glasses of lemonade. He muttered an apology and made to go around.

Suddenly, she had a plan.

She responded to his words with a simpering laugh. 'La, sir. It is a relief to see you. I retired to the corner for I was parched and near to fainting.'

Before he could offer or deny, she reached out and took two of his lemonades away from him, taking a sip from the first. 'Much better,' she said, giggling again and ignoring his astonishment at her rudeness.

Then, as if she was as unsteady as she claimed, she turned and staggered forward the two steps necessary to stand before Benjamin Lovell. She wavered, lurched and allowed herself a brief, triumphant smile. Then she dumped the contents of the glasses in her hand down his elegant white waistcoat.

Chapter Two

Damn it all to hell.

Ben Lovell was not given to outbursts of temper. Not in public, at least. Occasionally, when he was totally alone, he gave way to self-pity and cursed the strange turns his life had taken to land him where he was. Then he remembered that only a fool would complain over what must be seen by others as stunningly good luck, composed himself again, counted his blessings and ignored the rest.

In public he could allow nothing more than one brief, unspoken curse, making sure to give no indication on his face of displeasure within. Things had been going far too well for him to spoil his perfect reputation with a cross word towards the little idiot who had baptised him in lemonade.

This accident had ruined any chance for a meeting with Summoner tonight. If one wished to lay the groundwork for a political career, one could not afford to look less than one's best, or to appear out of sorts. One certainly could not have one's mind clouded with ill will over what was an innocent mistake by a flustered debutante.

For now, he would be a gentleman and ignore the ruined coat that had cost a full thirty pounds just the previous week. He would shake off the drips of lemonade falling from the thin picot of lace at the cuffs of his linen shirt. His cravat was a sodden lump and he could feel the hair on his chest sticking to his body. How many cups had the chit been carrying to result in such havoc? Had she been actively trying to drown him?

And where had she come from? He was normally careful to avoid treading on toes or bumping elbows even in the most crowded rout. She had seemed to appear out of nowhere, as if she'd been lying in wait to attack him.

A gentleman should not be bothered with trivia and Ben did not want to be known simply as well mannered. To overcome his birth, he must be the most magnanimous man in London.

He buried his annoyance and forced his face into an expression of concern for the lady. Then he reached for his handkerchief, holding the linen out to the giggling girl. She was flapping a broken fan as if she meant to dry him off with the breeze. 'I am so sorry to have startled you, miss. Did any of it spill upon your gown?' Then he looked down into the heart-shaped face barely level with his top vest button.

He was staring. It was rude of him. To be the success he wished to be, he could not afford to be anything less than perfect. But one look into that face and he was gaping like an idiot. All common sense seemed to have fled and taken his good manners with it.

It was not that she was a striking beauty. Pretty enough, he supposed. A fine figure, though she was none too tall. In an attempt to add height, her brown hair was piled in an overly fussy style with too many braids and curls. The plumes that completed her coiffure bobbed as she nodded her head along with his apology. Judging by the giggles, he assumed her head was likely full of feathers as well.

Or perhaps not.

Her laugh was so false and inane that it might have been cultivated to put a man off. But if she meant to be repellent, her eyes spoiled the effect. They drew him in and held him captive. They were large and bright, and the warm brown of a fine sherry. Or almost totally so. The left one had a single fleck of gold in the iris that glittered like a secret joke.

The difference between the two should have been unattractive for was not beauty dependent on symmetry? Instead, it was fascinating. He was lost in that little gold speck, enthralled by it. He wanted to gaze into her eyes forever, until they revealed their mysteries. Worse yet, as she looked into his eyes he was overcome with a desire to unburden himself and share even the most carefully concealed secrets of his past.

Then the feeling dissipated. On second look, what he had taken for mystique was a glimmer of calculation. He did not have to reveal his true self to her. Somehow, she had found him out and meant to punish him for his impudence. She was merely playing the simpering wallflower to disguise a dangerous, almost masculine intelligence.

'Thank you, sir, for your concern. My dress is undamaged. But your poor suit…' She dabbed at the liquid staining his lapels with a force guaranteed to drive the stuff deeper into the fabric.

He seized her gloved hand as gently as possible to stop the damage it was doing. 'That will not be necessary,' he said, firmly. 'But thank you for the attempt.'

'Oh, but, sir, I am so sorry.' She looked up at him with the melting gaze of a spaniel. The look appeared so suddenly that she must practise innocence in a mirror to produce it on cue. It left him all the more sure that she was not the least bit sorry. In fact, she enjoyed seeing him discommoded.

He gave her an equally practised smile. 'It is nothing. We will not speak of it again.' Because, God willing, he would never see her again. There was something far too disquieting about her. From now on, he would be on his guard and maintain a safe distance should they meet.

'Thank you.' She dropped a hurried curtsy and disappeared as suddenly as she had arrived.

Beside him, his friend laughed. 'Well done, sir.'

'Well done? I did nothing.' He wiped at the stains on his coat and then gave up, throwing the handkerchief aside.

'Apparently, you made an impression on Miss Summoner.'

Ben scanned the room for the pathway to his future. She was on the far side now, in conversation with the featherheaded chit who had doused him. Were they friends? No. There was something in the slant of their heads that spoke of a family likeness. 'Dear God, do not tell me...'

'Sisters,' Templeton said with another laugh. 'The little one is the elder. A spinster, from what people say.'

'I wonder why,' Ben said, not bothering to disguise his sarcasm.

'She claims she does not wish to marry and that she cannot be parted from her sister.'

'All women with an ounce of pride say something similar when they cannot get a husband,' Ben replied. 'It is far more likely that she behaved to others as she behaved to me and that society has taken a distaste of her.'

'It hardly matters,' Templeton said, quite reasonably. 'After several years, she is properly on the shelf. But if you want the younger, you had best get used to her. The elder Miss Summoner will likely be a member of your household after you are married.'

'She most certainly will not,' Ben said with a shudder of dread. Looking into those eyes at breakfast each morning would be no different from coming to the table naked. She would strip each defence from him, giggling all the while.

'Where else will she go?' Templeton said in the voice of reason. 'Lord Summoner will not live for ever. Then it will be up to her sister's husband to take her on.'

'Unless some unsuspecting gentlemen can be trapped into a union with her,' Ben suggested.

'What are the odds of that, after all this time on the market?'

'All this time?' Ben shot a quick look across the dance floor at her, then looked away before she could notice. 'She cannot be much more than three and twenty. That does not make her a crone, no matter what society might think. If one plucked her feathers and unbraided that hair, and perhaps chose a different dressmaker for her—' and taught her to hang on to her drinks and not to giggle so '—she would be quite pretty.'

'But the eye.' Templeton shuddered.

'Those eyes,' Ben corrected. 'She has two. And they are not unattractive. Just rather…startling.'

'What man wishes to be startled by a woman?' Templeton shuddered again. 'Perhaps you are greener than you pretend when it comes to the fair sex, Lovell. It is never good to be surprised by them.'

'Perhaps compelling is the word I am searching for. Or captivating.' Intoxicating. Fascinating. He could spend a lifetime trying to describe those eyes.

Templeton shook his head. 'Neither of those are as good as they sound, either. If you wish to be a puppet or a slave to a woman, then get yourself a mistress. Your days will be full of all the passion and melodrama you long for with no legal bonds to hold you when it grows tiresome.'

'I have no intention of living my life under the thumb of a woman, with or without marriage.'

Never again.

He continued. 'Nor do I think the elder Miss Summoner actually possesses the facility to dominate the man who marries her.' This last was not totally true. But the fact that he could imagine himself stripped bare and defenceless from a single glance might be nothing more than his own fears of the unhappy past repeating itself.

'If that is so, then there is no problem at all,' Templeton said, smiling. 'You seem to feel more than confident of controlling her. Though you do not wish to marry for love or passion, you admit you find her at least marginally attractive. If you wish a connection to Lord Summoner by marrying his daughter, Miss Amelia should be no different than Miss Arabella.'

Why not?

When presented with such a logical argument, he could not immediately think of an answer. Then he remembered the lemonade stain on his best waistcoat and the possibility of future social occasions marred by such accidents. If he wished to be thought unshakable, he could not attach himself to a woman who was constantly rattling his calm and spoiling his appearance. 'Only an idiot would pretend that the two Summoner daughters are interchangeable. Everyone in London admires the younger of the two. The elder is so far on the shelf that I did not even know of her existence. There is also the fact that I am seeking a wife who will be the picture of decorum and not an awkward wallflower. Belle Summoner glides through a room like a swan. And her sister…' He stared down at his ruined waistcoat.

Templeton laughed. 'You truly think that spill was an accident? My dear fellow, for all your polish, you are too naïve to survive the ladies of London.'

'Whatever do you mean?'

'Simply that if you come to Almack's and hide in the corner rather than standing up for a set, an interested female will try to get your attention by any means possible.'

This horrifying thought had not occurred to him. 'You think that…'

'She is smitten with you,' Templeton finished for him.

'And she did that on purpose to win my favour.' If that was true, then women truly were mad.

'There can be no other explanation for it. She fancies you. Since she is without prospects, I am sure Summoner will be all the more grateful to you for taking her off his hands.' Templeton clapped him on the shoulder. 'Go to him now and claim your prize.'

'I cannot go to him looking like this,' Ben said absently, staring across the room towards the woman who had attacked him. Could that have been the meaning of that glint in her eye? He had been sure there was some ulterior motive in her actions. But he'd have sworn it had less to do with marriage than a desire to unravel him like a fraying tapestry. 'I do not want to marry Miss Amelia,' he said, annoyed. He should not need to say those words aloud to clarify his intentions. If she was a spinster, the room was full of men who did not want her.

Templeton gave him a pitying look. 'You want Belle, as does every other man in London. But you have lost before you've begun, dear fellow. If you break her sister's heart with your indifference, Belle will have nothing to do with you. Women are like that, you know. They love each other more than they will ever love us.'

'Break her heart? I did nothing of the sort. I gave no indication that I was interested in her.' Unless she had seen something in the look he had given her. It had been but a glance, but it had seemed overlong, as if he had become lost in her eyes and needed to fight to get free.

'Of course not, Lovell.' The smirk on Templeton's face revealed the mockery in his assuring words. 'But I suggest you let Miss Amelia down as gently as possible. Then find another man she can affix herself to. If not, when you marry Belle, you will end with Amy Summoner permanently ensconced in your home, mooning over your lost love.'

Chapter Three

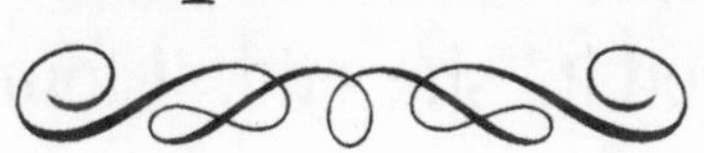

The next morning, Amy came down to her father's study, her list of prospective suitors in hand. In the matter of her sister's courtship and marriage, things were moving far too fast. The Season had barely begun, and total strangers like Benjamin Lovell were already mapping out Belle's future. The *laissez-faire* attitude that their father was bringing to a match might be acceptable for some girls, but not for Belle.

She rapped on the closed door and let herself in without waiting for an answer, then seated herself in the big leather chair in front of his desk.

Her father hardly looked up from his papers. 'You wish to speak to me, Amelia?'

'I wish to discuss last night's visit to Almack's.'

'I trust you both found it enjoyable.' The statement was a courtesy, nothing more. She could sense no real interest in it. Instead, there was the unspoken feeling that, since the fate of England hung on every decision he might make, Lord Summoner had no time for trivialities.

'Belle enjoyed it,' she said. 'I found it much the same as I always do.'

He sighed. 'Meaning you only bothered with it for your sister's sake. It is no wonder that you are not married. You make no effort.'

'I am not married because I found no one I could stand to spend a lifetime with,' she said, for what felt like the hundredth time.

'It is fortunate for me that your sister is not so particular.' He signed the document he had been reading and shook sand over the wet ink before setting it aside.

'Belle loves everyone. She does not know how to be particular,' Amy said. 'It will be up to us to choose wisely for her.'

'Us?' Her father looked up, fixing her with a quelling stare that she had long since learned to ignore.

'To that end,' she said, 'I took the time to evaluate the gentlemen at last night's ball, grading them according to their suitability.' She pushed the list across the desk to the empty space his documents had occupied.

He pushed it back without looking at it. 'You are overstepping yourself if you think to choose your sister's husband instead of your own.'

She could not help an unladylike snort. 'We have made progress, then. When I was actively searching, you were under the impression that the choice was yours alone.'

He sighed. 'And so it ought to have been. When your mother died, I allowed you far too much latitude and now I must pay the price for it.'

It was the way he chose to remember the past. When Mother died, he had not allowed or denied anything. He had simply gone to London and forgotten all about his daughters. 'It is fortunate that Arabella is more obedient,' she said.

'It is,' he agreed, taking no notice of the sarcasm in her voice.

Amy paused until she was sure that she had full control of her temper. 'I will admit that I have not been the sort of daughter you deserved. I am headstrong and wilful, but it does not mean I love you any less. Belle loves you as well. But we both know that she is not like other young ladies. It is why we must take care to protect her from those who might take advantage.'

Her father reached for another paper, nearly upsetting the inkwell in his eagerness to occupy his hands and mind with something other than the truth. 'Nonsense. If you did not coddle her so, there would be no problem. Perhaps I should have remarried. Then you would not have taken it upon yourself to mother her and she would have tried harder to catch up.'

'She tries very hard already,' Amy said, reaching out to touch her father's hand. 'And yet, there are many things she cannot manage. The doctors told you that her birth was difficult for both mother and child.'

'She was stronger than your mother,' he said stubbornly. 'Arabella survived.'

'But not unaffected,' Amy reminded him. 'She has always been slow to learn and easily confused.'

'She has as much wit as a woman needs to make a wife.'

'By that, I suppose you mean she has two arms, two legs and a smile,' she snapped.

'Her mother's smile,' he said reverently.

'She is beautiful,' Amy agreed, equally awed. It was as if God had given Belle a final blessing as he took her mother and her wits.

'And a pleasant disposition as well,' her father added. 'She is a sweet child, is she not?'

'Because we have never given her reason to be otherwise,' Amy reminded him. 'We have done all in our power to protect her. And we help her in those situations that she could not manage on her own.' The word *we* was an exaggeration. But it would gain her nothing to antagonise her father.

'Her life will not change so very much,' Lord Summoner said. 'I will find some young buck from a good family, with a decent fortune and a nice house. She will live in comfort for the rest of her life. And you will be free to do as you wish with your future, without troubling yourself over her.'

'I do not trouble myself,' Amy argued. 'Well,

not exactly.' It was sometimes difficult to have someone so dependent upon her. But it was even more difficult to think of Belle struggling without her. 'I love her,' she insisted. 'I help her when she needs it, because I want her to be happy.'

'Then you must not stand in the way of the marriage I will arrange for her.' Her father reached for another letter, breaking its wax seal with a swipe of his finger. It was a definitive gesture, meant to put an end to her argument.

Amy ignored it. 'An arranged marriage might be fine for some girls. But suppose her husband looks no further than her last name and does not understand that she cannot help the way she is?'

'He will find out, in time,' her father said. 'And by then, it will be too late to do anything about it.'

'You do not mean to explain?' Now Father sounded almost as heartless as Mr Lovell.

'An intelligent man will find it out for himself before he offers,' her father replied with another warning rattle of papers. 'If he does not, he will understand that marriages are negotiated contracts, no different than all other business. No human being is perfect. Both sides must balance advantages against defects before coming to an agreement.'

In her father's mind, the Summoner name had more than enough weight to balance the heaviest of problems. It was a shame that he did not want to marry Mr Lovell himself. They were well matched, since neither of them cared a fig for the feelings of the girl they would be bargaining over.

'Suppose the husband you choose does not love her as we do?'

'Love is not necessary before marriage. It might grow in time, of course.' When he looked up from his work, his expression was distant. 'I grew to be quite fond of your mother. Her loss was a blow from which I have yet to recover.' He cleared his throat. 'Mutual respect is a satisfactory basis for a relationship and far less painful for all parties involved.'

If that was his opinion, then the odious Mr Lovell was exactly the sort of son-in-law he was seeking. But how would she explain the abstract notions of a loveless union to her sister? 'It sounds very sensible. If we were discussing my courtship, I might be swayed. Belle is different. She will be happier in a match where there is mutual affection.'

'A romance, do you mean?' he responded with a condescending smile to remind her that, in comparison to a man, both his daughters were idiots. 'The fellow you are hoping for does not exist, Amelia. You have already admitted that your sister is unusual. We love her because we are her family. Others are not likely to be so charitable. Her future husband will require the inducements I am prepared to offer to overlook her deficiencies. It will not help her or any of us if you fill her head with nonsense.'

'It is not nonsense to want to love and be loved in return,' she said, wanting with all her heart to believe that was true.

Her father sighed. 'So you told me when you refused the offers put to you in your own Season. Now you seek to make a failure of your sister's come out.' He shook his head in disappointment. 'I did not think you so selfish, Amelia.'

'I am not selfish,' she insisted. 'I want what is best for her. If she weds, she will still need looking after. If you mean to choose a husband without a care to her feelings, it will be up to me to help her adjust to her new life and to console her should it all go wrong.'

His eyes narrowed, as if her words had only confirmed his opinion. 'I suspect your coddling the girl has caused most of her problems. When she does not have you to support her, she will learn to stand on her own, quick enough.'

'She will not because she cannot.' And thus they arrived at the usual sticking point. Discussions of Belle's difficulties always ended with her father refusing to believe they could not be solved by more effort on Belle's part and less interference on Amy's. 'This has nothing to do with desire to meddle in her future. She needs someone to care for her, Father. She always has. It is why I did not marry and why I intend to live in her household, after she weds. She needs me.'

Lord Summoner passed a hand over his brow to shield himself from feminine logic. 'It is one thing to play the spinster, Amelia, and quite another to actually become one. If you seriously think to follow her into her new household, I will have to find one man willing to take responsibility for both daughters. You are making my job twice as difficult.'

'Good,' she said, raising her chin in defiance. 'It will give me time to find her a man who truly understands her.'

'If the situation is as dire as you claim, then perhaps I should find a nurse for her and a husband for you.' It was a reasonable suggestion, but his cynical smile as he spoke revealed his true feelings in the matter. 'Since you have spent years ruining all chances for your own marriage that is now quite impossible. In any case, know that I cannot die leaving two unmarried daughters to fend for themselves.'

'Since you are not near to death, we hardly need to worry about it,' she pointed out, unwilling to respond to the bait he set for her.

'And you are not the head of the family, though you seem to think you can act thus. The final decision on Belle's future is mine and mine alone. She will be married by Season's end and your approval of my choice is not required or appreciated.'

He stood to indicate the interview was at an end, leaving her little choice but to leave the study, return to her room and plan her counter-attack.

Chapter Four

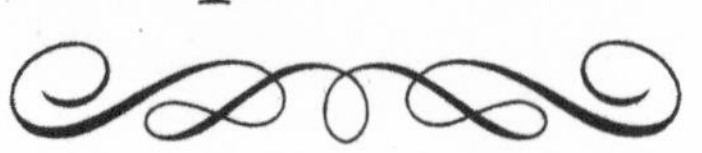

The difficult morning discussion was followed by an afternoon too beautiful to stay indoors. If Amy wished to circumvent her father's plans, there was no better place to spend it than on Rotten Row, where anyone of importance took to horse or carriage to see and be seen by the rest of the *ton*.

Belle was seated on her gentle, brown mare, looking her best in a bright blue riding habit with a tall hat dressed in lace. With hair of spun gold and eyes as blue as a summer sky, there was none to compare to her.

It was a shame.

As she did, each time the thought crossed her mind, Amy felt guilty and silently enumerated a few more of Belle's virtues. She was kind and loving. She was loyal and had a gentle heart. In comparison to all that, did her deficiencies amount to so much?

'I like to ride,' Belle said. Her hands stroked the horse's mane.

'As do I, dear,' Amy agreed and adjusted her own grip on her sister's reins to better lead her horse. 'Did you have a nice time at Almack's last night?'

'Yes,' Belle replied. 'I like to dance.'

'Did you speak with anyone of interest?' she probed gently.

As she tried to form an answer, Belle's smile dimmed. Thoughts flitted across her face like clouds. Then she smiled again. 'I danced every dance.'

'But with no gentleman more than once, I hope.' She had kept a close watch on Belle's dance card to prevent any partner from monopolising her time. But Belle, Lord bless her, was exceptionally easy to trick.

'I danced every dance,' she repeated, still smiling.

'You did, indeed,' Amy said, sighing.

'Will there be dancing at the wedding?'

'What wedding, dear?'

'My wedding.' There was much that her little sister did not understand. But she had grasped the main purpose of the Season. It was left to Amy to help her with the details.

'Weddings are held in the morning, Belle. There will be a breakfast, not a ball.'

'Oh.'

'But we must be sure that your husband likes to dance as much as you do.'

Belle nodded, satisfied. 'Who is he?'

'Your husband?' It had been too much to hope that Belle could understand her need to participate in the process of choosing such the man. 'We do not know as yet. We cannot choose just any man. We are looking for someone whose company you enjoy. Is there anyone you particularly liked last evening?'

'I liked the dancing,' she repeated again. 'And I liked all the boys who danced with me.'

Good-hearted soul that she was, Belle liked them all equally. Amy sighed again. 'I am making a list of gentlemen who might be good husbands. I have talked to Father about them.' And enough said about that, since there was no point in spoiling this conversation with the truth. 'We will find someone who loves you as much as we do.'

'Someone who likes to dance,' Belle added.

'Most definitely,' Amy agreed.

'And who likes dogs,' Belle added.

'Definitely,' Amy agreed. In her experience, all men loved dogs. Unfortunately, it was often a matter of like being drawn to like. 'But if there is any man you meet who likes dogs and dancing, and who you favour above others, you must tell us of him, immediately.'

'Everyone was nice to me,' Belle said, her smile as bright as ever. If she had a current favourite, she gave no indication of it. On their next outing, Amy would need to watch carefully for any signs of a preference that could be guided into something more.

For now, she must pay attention to the horses. She gave a gentle pull on the reins to slow them so they did not overtake two gentlemen who were stopped on the path ahead. Instead of resuming their ride as the girls approached, the men turned their mounts to look back at them.

In front of them, blocking their way, was the person she least wanted Belle to meet. Mr Lovell rode a dapple-grey stallion every bit as perfect as he was. And as usual, he was the picture of masculine perfection. He sat the horse as if he'd been born in its saddle. His hacking jacket and breeches stretched over muscles that he had not got from leisurely rides in Hyde Park. Rich, handsome and athletic.

She must stop ogling him and remember that he had designs on her sister. That meant he was also as loathsome as the snake in Eden. Amy sighed in frustration. She could not very well cut him without risk of offending Mr Templeton, who figured prominently on her list of acceptable suitors. It was a shame that such a fine gentleman had such horrible taste in friends.

'Miss Summoner. Miss Arabella.' Mr Templeton tipped his hat and gave them a smile that was soft and welcoming.

'Mr Templeton,' Amy replied with a smile and ignored the other man.

Beside her, she could sense Belle's confusion.

'We danced la Boulanger last night at Almack's,' Templeton supplied to remind her.

'And a Scottish reel last week,' Belle said, with a surprised smile.

She could not possibly be as surprised as Amy. The single sentence was more than Belle had spoken outside the family in ages.

'You remember me because I stepped on your toe,' he said, with a proud nod.

'Both times,' she said, nodding back happily.

There was a moment of silence as the gentlemen experienced the full effect of Miss Summoner's smile and were left dazed. Then Mr Templeton regained his composure. 'Last night, you left us so quickly I did not have the opportunity to introduce my friend, Mr Lovell.'

Belle's face registered her panic as she tried to remember the name and choose an appropriate response. In the end, she simply gave the other man a puzzled nod and another smile.

Amy had hoped an introduction to this scoundrel could be delayed until her sister had been directed towards an acceptable suitor. Now, she must pray that Belle forgot Lovell, as she did so many others who'd crossed her path so far this Season. Or perhaps he would realise that he was not wanted and simply go away. Amy gave him a frosty nod of acknowledgement. 'Mr Lovell.'

'Are you ladies enjoying your ride?' Was she mistaken, or was the smile Lovell offered to Belle more intense than the one he offered her? Given the plans she'd overheard, it was not surprising. It made no sense that Amy should care one way or the other about the lack of attention directed her way.

Belle was silent, but it did not matter. Amy was accustomed to speaking for both of them. 'We like it very well, sir.'

'We must not block the path with our chat,' Templeton said, still smiling. 'Miss Arabella, would you care to ride ahead with me and allow Mr Lovell to escort your sister?'

Belle gave her a look that was half-hopeful, and half-fearful. The larger the group, the more confused she became. But it appeared that she was accustomed to speaking with Templeton. Or, at least, she did not mind listening to him. Amy gave her an encouraging nod and offered Belle's reins to him as she manoeuvred her own horse backwards.

With a triumphant smile, Templeton took control of her sister's mount and the pair trotted a few steps ahead so they might converse in private.

Did she see a flicker of annoyance on Lovell's face at being so quickly cut out of his first conversation with Belle? Or was it merely a shadow from the leaves on a nearby branch? When Amy looked again, he was all pleasantness, as if it had been his intention all along to ride at her side instead. 'Miss Summoner?' He tilted his head, indicating that they hurry to catch up.

Amy slackened her grip on the reins and let her horse proceed at a leisurely walk.

Ahead of them, things seemed to be going well. She could hear Templeton droning on about something that evoked a delighted laugh from Belle. But between her and Lovell there was a silence that would have been uncomfortable had she wanted to speak to him, which she did not.

'It is a lovely day for a ride,' he said, when he was unable to bear it any longer.

'Yes,' she agreed. 'It is.'

'And that is a very...serviceable habit you have on today.'

She smiled. Next to Belle's her costume was hardly a fashion plate. When they went on these little outings, it was usually her job to manage both horses while giving Belle an illusion of control. But it left Amy little energy to fuss over her appearance. Her current ensemble was dark green and devoid of ornament, except for a muddy footprint at the hem that had been gained when she'd ridden too close to Belle's horse and scraped against the stirrup. Despite his excellent manners, Mr Lovell could not bring himself to lie and call it pretty.

'It suits me well enough,' she replied, staring down at a loose button on the sleeve.

'If I may be so bold as to suggest it, a little lace at the cuffs might be quite flattering.'

She snapped her head up to look at him. 'Are you a dressmaker, Mr Lovell, that you question the design of my clothing?'

'Merely making an observation,' he said blandly. 'Miss Arabella is most fetchingly attired. You cannot expect gentlemen to notice you if you insist on standing in your sister's shadow.'

Now she was not just looking at him, she was staring. 'If you mean to offer me insults in the guise of friendly advice, please refrain, sir. I am quite content with both my sister's popularity and my choice of attire.'

'And your lack of escort?' he said.

'Lack of escort?' She looked around, pretending surprise. 'Correct me if I am mistaken, but are you not escorting me at this very moment? Or is this some fever dream that I've concocted featuring a man I've just met?'

'You met me yesterday,' he reminded her. 'There was no formal introduction, of course.'

She gave him a blank look, pretending to forget.

'You spilled your drink on me last night at Almack's,' he prompted.

'Of course,' she said, giving him a smile that was as overly sweet as the lemonade had been. 'I apologised. And you said we would not speak of it again.'

He gave a dismissive shrug, as if to say the circumstances had changed now that he knew her identity.

'And it was two drinks,' she prodded.

He responded with such benign sympathy that it made her wish for a pitcher of the stuff so she might pour the whole of it over his insufferable head. 'It was not necessary to do that to achieve this meeting,' he said. 'I would have been more than willing to ride with you even if you had not wasted two glasses of lemonade on my new waistcoat.'

'You think I did that on purpose?' she said, outraged. Of course, she had done it on purpose. But somehow, he had got the idiotic idea that it had been a ploy to gain his attention.

'I think there are some young ladies who take naturally to society. And the *ton* rewards them for it.' He cast a brief, longing look forward at her sister, before turning back to her. 'While others, even though they are blest with many of the same gifts, lack a certain something.' He shrugged. 'Confidence, perhaps? That natural ease amongst people. As a result, they are quite unfairly overlooked by gentlemen when it comes time to marry.'

She bit her lip before she could blurt that her sister's inability to string two sentences together was not actually feminine wisdom masking some sort of magical self-assurance. It was as she'd often suspected: though some might call Belle a fool, it was the men chasing her who were the idiots. And she was speaking to their king. 'Suppose these poor, neglected unfortunates you describe are quite happy with their lot?' Her tone rose slightly. 'Perhaps, having met the gentlemen of London society, they would much rather remain single than spend the rest of their lives pretending an unworthy man is not just their equal, but their divinely ordained superior?'

Now she definitely saw anger in his eyes, but it was stifled almost as quickly as his earlier annoyance. He sucked in his lips for a moment, biting back the words he wanted to say, burying his true feelings. He was clever enough to think before he spoke. But it proved his amiable courtesy was little more than a thin veneer that might peel away if she continued to pry at it.

'Then…' he said, pausing again, 'I would say that…' another pause '…if they were truly content with their unmarried status, they would not find it necessary to giggle unceasingly, to flap their fans like deranged parrots and orchestrate accidents to call attention to themselves.'

'Accidents like this, you mean?' She brought her riding crop down in one swift motion, slapping the tip of it against his horse's flank with a force equivalent to a wasp sting.

The enormous grey obliged with an irate whinny and reared.

His rider, who had been far too occupied with whatever condescending response he had been composing in his head, lost his grip on the reins and landed on the tan-covered trail behind his horse.

A few heads turned to stare at the man sitting in the mud. But not nearly enough of them, in Amy's opinion. This minor embarrassment might go largely unnoticed if she did not help it along. 'Mr Templeton,' she sang out in a shrieking soprano. 'Oh, dear. Mr Templeton! Mr Lovell has fallen from his horse! Someone help him, I pray.'

'I am fine.' He stood to prove the fact, one hand in the air in a self-deprecating wave to show the mildest embarrassment. But she was close enough to hear shattered pride in each of the three words. He followed them with a wry smile and an admonition. 'Really, Miss Summoner. Do not distress yourself on my account. There is nothing to worry about.'

But the look he gave her said something far different.

You have nothing to worry about, yet.

Chapter Five

Ben stared out of the window of his rooms at the busy crowds below him on Bond Street, contemplating his future. Hopefully, it would be devoid of the humiliation he had experienced on yesterday's ride in Hyde Park.

He was an expert horseman, able to handle even the most spirited cattle with ease. But after five minutes of conversation with Miss Amelia Summoner he had been displayed before all of London society as a man who could not hold his seat on a walk down a bridle path. Worst of all, her sister had turned back to see him muddied and bruised. Her laughter at his predicament was a hundred times more painful than the fall had been.

If the experience in Rotten Row had gained him anything, it was proof that his friend Templeton was only partly correct in his assessment of Miss Summoner. Ben could see no sign that she was romantically attracted to him or anyone else. But it seemed that she was, in some way, obsessed with him. Her fixation bordered almost on mania. Could it be an untreated madness, or was there something he had done to set her off? He could not think what that might be. She had seemed set against him, even before an introduction was made. Perhaps she had chosen him at random to bear the brunt of her jealousy over her sister's success. Or maybe she simply hated men.

After ten years in the thrall of one, he was more than wary of the focused attentions of overly clever women. At first he had been drawn to Cassandra's intellect and aspired to become her equal. To be worthy of such a woman, a man had to strive for constant improvement.

The day had come when he'd finally been ready for the verbal fencing matches he'd dreamed of. He'd honed his wits to a rapier point only to discover she was wielding a stiletto. She had made him suffer for his impudence in believing he could ever be her master.

Never again.

Such women might make the best mistresses. Like the mote in Miss Amelia's eye, even their flaws seemed to sparkle with a tempting vivacity. But now that he meant to marry, it would be to the quiet beauty of an Arabella. It would be like coming home to a house filled with fresh flowers, each day. Just the thought of her smile made the tensions in his soul relax. After what he had been through, he deserved peace.

It did not matter what fate Amelia Summoner planned for him. He wanted no part of it. But in one thing, his friend Templeton, had been totally right. To gain the ultimate tranquillity of a life with Belle, Ben would need to douse the conflagration that burned in her sister. If the elder of the two became a member of his household, his life would be far more difficult than he wished it to be. There must be some man in London who could take her off his hands.

First, he must find a way to charm her out of the irrational antipathy she displayed towards him. Once a truce had been declared, perhaps, he could gain some insight into her character and find an acceptable match for her where Lord Summoner had failed. He took a moment to imagine the happy gratitude of that gentleman at settling a matter that no doubt weighed heavily on his mind. It would be one more thing that would smooth the way when Ben asked for his younger daughter's hand.

And there, on the street just below him, were the two women he most wanted to impress, admiring the bonnets in the milliner's shop opposite his rooms. The older woman who accompanied them, and who he assumed was their chaperon, was swaying slightly as the terrier on the leash in her hand strained at each passer-by.

Perhaps today he might make an impression on the pair of them without Templeton swooping in to monopolise Arabella. Ben gave a brief glance in the mirror to assure himself that his cravat and coat were spotless before racing down the stairs. At the door, he took only a moment to compose himself again, so that their meeting might seem a chance encounter on London's most popular shopping thoroughfare.

But in the moments it had taken to get from

sitting room to street, his future wife had disappeared along with her keeper, leaving Miss Amelia and the dog as grim sentinels prepared to thwart his plans.

The girl glanced in his direction for only a moment, before turning back to stare at the shop window in a deliberate attempt to ignore him. The terrier, however, pivoted on the line holding him to give Ben's shoes a thorough sniffing. The little beast was uncommonly ugly for a lady's pet. It seemed to be made of the parts of a variety of animals, stuck together in a haphazard fashion by someone who had no clear idea of what a dog was supposed to look like. Its long body supported an enormous head and waddled along on hardly any legs at all. The whole of it was covered with a layer of unevenly cropped white-and-tan fur. When it had completed its investigation of his shoes, it looked up at him with an air of resigned embarrassment at its own appearance. It was then he saw that its eyes were no more coordinated than the rest of it. They were large as a bug's and mismatched in colour, one blue, one brown, like a ridiculous parody of the woman who controlled it. It ambled forward and flopped down upon his foot, giving him far more notice than its owner, who was still stubbornly ignoring him.

If he meant to join her family, he could not allow her to cut him on the street. He nudged the dog gently aside and stepped forward, smiling. 'Miss Summoner.'

He was sure he had spoken loud enough to be heard, but she remained purposefully oblivious.

'Miss Summoner,' he said more loudly to prove he would not be denied. Then he took his place beside her, trying to meet her eyes in the reflection of the glass.

She did not turn, still focusing on the goods displayed. 'You are not the gentleman you claim to be, Mr Lovell.'

Her words hit so close to the truth that his smile faltered and he bit his tongue to stop the question echoing in his head.

What have you heard?

She continued with the obvious explanation for her words. 'Surely you know that when a lady does not acknowledge you, you must not persist in trying to engage her.'

It was nothing. He was safe. He let out a relieved breath and shifted his leg to detach the dog, who was now sniffing the hems of his pants. 'Have I done something to offend you?' he asked, honestly curious.

'To offend me? No, Mr Lovell, you have not. But I would hate to spoil that.'

'Do not be glib with me, Miss Summoner.'

'I was not attempting to be,' she reminded him. 'I was attempting to avoid you.'

'But why?' Now he sounded like a petulant child. He gave her reflection another disarming smile. 'Is there a reason that we cannot have a friendly conversation when we meet on a crowded street?'

She gave him a governess's sigh of disappointment. 'Let us be honest, just for a moment. You do not want to speak to me, Mr Lovell. You wish to speak to my sister.'

Did she honestly think he would be rude enough to admit the truth? He glanced around him. 'Then I will be sorely disappointed. She is not here at the moment.'

'Because she has gone to Gunter's for an ice.'

He could not help himself. His head turned in the direction of the confectioner's shop, revealing his true motive. To hide his embarrassment, he bent down to pet the dog, carefully removing the sodden fabric of his pants leg from the animal's mouth. Then he looked down at Miss Amelia, all innocence. 'There is no reason I cannot speak to both of you.'

'Now who is being glib, Mr Lovell? Your desire to be all things to all people puts me in mind of a politician. Perhaps it is my father you should be talking to instead of Belle and me.'

Was the woman really so astute as to guess his plans, or were his motives transparent? Either way, if he denied it now, she would have reason to call him a liar when the truth became clear. He gave her what he hoped was a winning smile. 'I will take that as a compliment, Miss Summoner. I would consider it an honour to serve my country by standing for office.'

She responded to this with a shudder of revulsion that surprised him.

'I would think you, of all people, would have respect for public servants,' he said.

'Because of my father?' She let out a brief sharp laugh. 'I stand corrected, Mr Lovell. You are far too naïve for politics.'

If he was being naïve, it would not be the first time. 'Perhaps I am. But that will not keep me from seeking a seat in the House of Commons. It will do more good than harm to have members willing to effect changes to benefit the common men our government supposedly represents.'

'A reformer?' Her brows rose, making her eyes seem even larger. 'I can hardly wait for you to meet my father, Mr Lovell. He will eat you and your ambitions for breakfast.'

Some small part of him quailed at the thought that a man who might be so instrumental to his future could end it before he'd even begun. But he had come too far to quit without so much as an attempt, based on the word of a woman who seemed almost desperate to thwart him. 'Then I shall work to be so palatable that he digests my ideas and makes them his own,' he replied.

For the first time, she looked at him with what almost appeared to be admiration.

Emboldened, he went on. 'And for your information, Miss Summoner, I do not consider myself a reformer. The modern machines found in the factories of the north have workers in an uproar. Soldiers who loyally served their King and country return from our wars missing limbs and with no means of supporting themselves beyond begging. Society changes with or without our help. We must be ready to guide it when it does or the country will fall to ruin.'

She clapped her gloved hands in mock admiration, causing the dog at his feet to release his leg and retreat behind her skirts. 'Bravo, Mr Lovell. What a stirring speech. But it was hardly necessary to give it to me. The elections for the position you seek are, for the most part, forgone conclusions.'

'The votes are controlled by men like your father,' he agreed. 'But that does not mean I do not belong in government, nor will it stop me from trying to win your favour. Were you able to vote, perhaps you might agree with some of my positions.'

'Perhaps I would. I at least agree with your position that our country should be concerned with the welfare of the weak as well as the strong.' She shrugged dismissively. 'If I have grown cynical over the likelihood of that happening, it is the world and my father that have made me so.'

There was something in the unwavering and intelligent gaze she returned that made him wonder if he might be better off if Amelia Summoner could vote. Perhaps, if her quick wits were acknowledged and put to use, she would not be using them to bedevil the men in her life.

'Let us call a truce, then,' he said. 'I acknowledge that my behaviour has been abominable, demanding that you speak to me when you clearly did not want to. I should not have done so.'

At this, she turned to look at him and he saw the faintest shift in the fleck of her eye, as if deep waters had been stirred to give a glimpse of what rested beneath. 'And I had no right to mock your ambitions. They are noble ones, though I suspect they are doomed to failure.' Then the vulnerability was gone and she was just as hard and brittle as she always was. 'But that does not mean I will allow you access to my sister. You can want only two things in gaining an introduction to her.'

'Really?' he said, his apology forgotten and sarcasm coming to the fore again. 'Enlighten me.'

'You either seek a dishonourable liaison...'

'Dishonourable?' He blew his breath out in a great puff that would have been a curse if he had not been in the company of a lady. The terrier reappeared and gave a low growl to remind him of his manners. 'I can assure you I would never intend such a thing.'

'Then you are thinking of marriage,' Miss Amelia said, tipping her head to the side as she looked at him, as if observing some exotic creature. 'Since that is not to be, it hardly seems necessary for you to seek her out for a deeper acquaintance.'

'I have barely spoken to her yet. How, exactly, would you know that there is no hope?' he asked. Then he studied her just as closely as she did him. 'Are the lady's affections fixed upon another?'

'To the best of my knowledge, they are not,' she said. 'But the lack of a rival does not automatically make you a good candidate for husband.'

'Nor should it exclude me,' he replied, doing his best to be perfectly reasonable. 'I ask again, have I done something to make you set against a possible match?'

Again, he saw the movement in the depths. And again, it resulted in nothing. 'I know her. And I know you.'

'You hardly know me at all,' he reminded her. 'We have just met.'

'I know you well enough to see that you will not suit,' she countered.

He swallowed his denial. Could she really see past the façade so easily and know that he was unworthy?

'I know that you are exactly like all the other gentlemen of the *ton,*' she finished.

So it was nothing about him that she specifically disliked. 'Then you have a problem with males in general,' he said.

'Not at all.' She gave a slow, cat-like blink of her mismatched eyes. 'I merely think that you are ordinary. My sister will require the extraordinary.'

The last word touched him like a finger drawn down his spine. His mind argued that she was right. There was nothing the least bit exceptional about him. If she learned the truth, she would think him common as muck and far beneath her notice. But then, he remembered just how far a man could rise with diligence and the help of a beautiful woman. He leaned in to her, offering his most seductive smile. 'Then I shall simply have to be extraordinary for you.'

For Arabella.

That was what he had meant to say. He was supposed to be winning the princess, not flirting with the gatekeeper. But he had looked into those eyes again and had lost his way.

She showed no sign of noticing his mistake. Or had her cheeks gone pink? It was not much of a blush, just the barest hint of colour to imply that she might wish him to be as wonderful as he claimed.

In turn, he felt a growing need to impress her, to see the glow kindle into warm approval. Would her eyes soften when she smiled, or would they sparkle? And what would they do if he kissed her?

He blinked. It did not matter. His words had been a simple mistake and such thoughts were an even bigger one. They had not been discussing her at all. And now her dog was tugging on his pants again, as if to remind him that he should not, even for an instant, forget the prize he had fixed his sights on from the first.

She shook her head, as if she, too, needed to remember the object of the conversation. 'If you must try to be extraordinary, Mr Lovell, then you have failed already. You either are, or you aren't.'

He gave another shake of his leg, trying to dislodge the animal, and glared down at her. 'So you think a man who is not born as pure as Galahad is not worthy to marry into your family.'

'That is not what I meant and you know it.'

Then she had heard the lie everyone believed about his parentage, judged him by it and found him wanting. If illegitimacy shocked her, how distasteful would she find the truth? 'Is your view of the world really so narrow that you cannot acknowledge a man might rise above his birth and endeavour to improve his character when he sees deficiency in it?'

She glanced away from him, down the street towards the confectioner's shop where her sister must have gone. 'My view is not the least bit narrow. But I know for a fact that there are some obstacles that cannot be overcome by wanting, Mr Lovell. You are not the right man for my sister and that is that.'

He had been foolish enough to speak of his ambitions and she'd seemed to agree. But apparently he was still not good enough. Not for her or her precious sister. He gave her a pitying smile. 'While it is kind of you to want the best for her, perhaps you should let Miss Arabella choose her own husband and tend to your own future. If she is just down the street, there is no reason I cannot meet with her now and see what she thinks of me.'

'Don't you dare.' Amelia glared back at him, like a five-foot three-inch pillar of fire. 'Your fine and idealistic talk is nothing more than that, Mr Lovell. Nothing but words. And I will not have you making sheep's eyes at Arabella, only to abandon her when your conquest has been successful. Leave her alone or I shall set the dog upon you.'

The animal in question was still tugging at him, as if to emphasise his mistress's words. Ben gave a yank and heard cloth rip as his pants leg tore. When he looked down, her dog was holding a piece of his best pantaloons between its crooked teeth, tail wagging furiously as if he expected a reward.

For a moment, his temper got the better of him and he grabbed the scrap of cloth from its mouth, glaring at the girl who held the leash. 'Miss Summoner, if you cannot control this miserable cur, then you should not bring him out in public to trouble the rest of us.'

Miss Amelia looked down at the dog with a triumphant smile. 'Good dog, Mellie. You see him for what he is, don't you? A man who does not care one bit for our Belle. If he did, he would know that you are not a miserable cur. You are Belle's best friend in the world.'

Then she looked back at him, her smile disappearing. 'Belle has very few requirements of the men who court her, Mr Lovell. She has requested someone who likes both dancing and dogs. When you were at Almack's, a place where there is little else to do but stand up for a set, you did nothing but stand at the side of the room and speculate on others.'

'You cannot mean to judge me on a single evening,' he countered.

She gave no quarter. 'It is plain from your opinion of Mellie that you have failed in the second requirement as well.'

'I like dogs,' he argued. Perhaps not this one. But it was hardly the standard bearer of its kind. 'I like them as well as any man.'

'But they do not like you,' she said. 'And neither do I.' She gave a sharp tug on the leash and abandoned him to find her sister.

Chapter Six

Amy sat with her sister in the parlour of the Summoner town house, waiting for the maid to bring their tea. Their shopping trip that afternoon had been, for want of a better word, illuminating. To his credit, Mr Lovell had made no effort to hide his ambitions and his views did him credit. He would make an admirable politician and, perhaps, if he was not ground down by bitter reality, he would do the world some good.

The earnestness of his manner as he had talked of the future had come close to breaching the barricades she had created between herself and the masculine sex. Here was a man she might like to talk to and who was willing to treat her like something more than a silly girl who was Summoner's daughter.

And when he had looked into her eyes…

It was an autonomic reaction on her part, more biological than rational. He was pleasant to look at and quick witted. When he turned his full attention on her, it was only logical that she became flustered. If his plans had involved her and not her sister, Amy might even have liked him.

But they did not. He wanted Belle. And Amy had only to look at their father to know that a politician would be the worst type of husband for Arabella. The eyes of such men were ever on the horizon and their minds were fixed on the future. It left no time or interest for the problems in their own homes, right under their very noses.

To his credit, he was persistent. She doubted he was ready to concede. In another man, such unwavering devotion would have been a virtue. But his cold-blooded approach to courtship ruined everything. Her attempts thus far had done nothing to put him off. She must have a better plan in place before their next meeting.

She glanced over at her sister and smiled. 'How is your needlework coming?'

'It is done.' Belle handed her the handkerchief

she had been hemming, picked up Mellie from his place on the floor at her feet and scratched his ears.

Amy glanced at the row of uneven stitches, then moved it over to her pile to rip and redo.

'I tried,' Belle said, more to the dog than to anyone else. Then she gave Amy the worried, frustrated look that she sometimes got when forced to do a thing that was beyond her ability. 'Is it good?'

'You did your best.' Amy gave her an encouraging smile in return and watched as her sister's brow unfurrowed. She had tried. But years of watching had taught Amy her sister's limitations. It did no good to try and push her past them.

'I don't like sewing,' Belle said, gathering the terrier in a hug and being rewarded by a lick on the nose.

Amy nodded sympathetically. 'You must try, for Father's sake. He says it is important that young ladies know such things.'

'Maybe my husband will know how to sew,' Belle said, using her embroidery scissors to trim the stray locks of hair that were obscuring Mellie's mismatched eyes.

Amy sighed. It would be far easier to find a man in London capable of sewing a button that did not immediately fall off than to teach Belle to do it. 'Instead, we will find you a husband who does not care who does the mending.' Then a thought struck her. 'And, in case he should ask, I do not think you should marry Mr Lovell. When I saw him on Bond Street, he had holes in his trousers that needed fixing.'

'I do not know how to do that,' Belle said, frowning.

'Neither do I,' Amy assured her. Short of turning them into knee breeches, she suspected the aforementioned garments were a total loss. In gratitude, she took a biscuit from the plate on the table between them, tossed it to Mellie and added, 'Also, he did not like dogs.'

'Then I do not like him.' Belle frowned. 'Which one is Mr Lovell?'

The fact that he had already been forgotten made Amy regret introducing him into the conversation. 'The man who fell off his horse in Hyde Park.'

Belle smiled. 'He looked very funny.'

Amy toyed, for a moment, with the idea of reminding her sister that it was not kind to laugh at the unfortunate. Then she answered, 'Yes, he did. And you must trust me to know what is best for you. You would not be happy married to a man like that, even if he is funny.'

Now her sister's lips pursed, ever so slightly, as she tried to imagine what it might be like to be unhappy. All the more reason that Amy must care for her. While she might have no trouble imagining circumstances that were less than ideal, Belle really had no idea what that would be like.

After a long pause, Belle spoke. 'I think I would like to marry Mr Templeton.'

The words came as such a surprise that Amy stabbed her finger with the needle. She jammed the injured digit into her mouth, to forestall a response until she had chosen the correct words.

Belle took advantage of the silence to tell her more. 'Mr Templeton has no holes in his clothes and has promised to bring a ball for Mellie when I take him to the park.'

Amy pulled her finger out of her mouth and shook the sting from it. 'Mr Templeton is a fine gentleman. He seems very pleasant.' He was also near the top of her list of candidates and seemed to enjoy her sister's company even though he must have some clue by now as to her difficulties.

Belle smiled and patted her dog. 'The next time I see him, I will ask him to marry me.'

This resulted in another missed stitch and poked finger. 'You will do no such thing.'

'Why?' Belle was staring at her with wide, guileless eyes, probably fearing that she was to be scolded for yet another thing she did not understand.

Amy took care to moderate her tone and smile, as she delivered her explanation. 'Ladies do not do the asking.'

'I am better at talking than at sewing,' Belle reminded her.

'Yes, you are. All the same, you must wait for Mr Templeton to decide that he wants to marry you. If he does, he will ask you. Then he will talk to Father about it. And then…'

Her sister's eyes were beginning to glaze, lost in the many steps between her and an absolutely perfect solution.

Amy reached out and patted her hand. 'Your way would be easier, but it is just not done. Do not worry. I will help you discover his intentions and it will be settled in no time at all. Perhaps we will see him tonight, at the Middletons' musicale.'

Lord and Lady Middleton's entertainments were a favourite of Belle, who loved anything to do with music. But since they were usually concerts with no dancing, the crowds tended to be smaller, older and more sedate than those at Almack's. Guests sat for the majority of the evening in rigidly arranged gilt chairs listening to the musicians before partaking of the cold supper at midnight. If the Summoner girls left early, there was little time for conversation, which worked to Belle's advantage. And by careful selection of seating, Amy was able to control her companions.

Tonight she seated Belle on the aisle and near the front. From there, her sister would have a clear view of the soprano performing and no gentleman would dare drag a chair to sit on her opposite side without calling undue attention to his actions and blocking the way for others. Amy took the seat on her other side, watching the door for the appearance of Mr Templeton. She meant to hold the place until he arrived. Then she would find an excuse to go to the ladies' retiring room, yielding the chair to him so he might spend the rest of the evening beside her sister. It would be far easier to encourage the right man than to battle a slew of wrong ones.

The performance was almost ready to begin. Lady Middleton was talking to the accompanist and Belle was facing front, printed programme clutched in eager hands, ready for the first song. But despite Lord Middleton's assurance that he was expected, there had been no sign of Mr Templeton.

Amy was almost ready to give up when she heard a commotion in the hall and the sound of a man's voice, apologising for his lateness. It was him! She touched her sister's shoulder in apology and was out of her seat and halfway down the aisle before she realised the truth.

Mr Lovell stood in the doorway to the room, scanning the crowd for an empty chair. By leaving hers, she had played directly into his hands, all but saving the perfect seat for him. Past him, she heard the sound of another latecomer. Certainly, that was Mr Templeton. If it was not, any other man would be a better companion than the one she had been trying to discourage. What was she to do?

She continued forward blindly, pretending she did not notice him, though she could see through the lashes of her downcast eyes that his mouth was open, ready to greet her. When she was barely an arm's length away, she feigned a swoon.

His fingers closed around her upper arm in support catching her before she collapsed. 'Amelia.' His urgent whisper of concern sounded surprisingly sincere.

'Please,' she whispered back. 'Help me from the room. The air is so close. The heat…' It was neither warm nor stuffy in the music room. If anything, she was glad of her shawl. But he had not been there long enough to notice, nor did he show any signs of questioning her distress.

Instead, he maintained his grip on her arm, turning to add a gentlemanly hand at the centre of her back as he escorted her from the room. A footman who was dealing with Mr Templeton's hat and stick leaned in, ready to help.

Amy waved him away with a gloved hand and then gestured to the other late arrival. 'Please, Mr Templeton,' she said, fluttering her lashes as though struggling to remain conscious. 'See to my sister. She is alone at the front of the room.'

Mr Templeton hesitated, ready to help her instead.

She shook her head and, as they passed him, she gave a sharp jerk of her head to indicate that he go immediately to the place he really wanted to be. Then she followed it with an annoyed roll of her eyes to the man at her side.

Mr Lovell was too busy ushering her forward to notice this silent communication. But clearly, Mr Templeton understood. He responded with a slow smile and a nod of thanks before turning towards the music room so he might take her unoccupied chair.

Now that he was settled, she must figure out how to free herself from the situation she had created with Mr Lovell. It was a large house. Large enough to hide a body in, she thought with a grim smile. She need do nothing as dire as that. She just had to find an empty room with a key still in the door, or a chair that might be propped under a handle to detain this troublemaker.

'I will find someone to help you.' He looked around. 'A maid, perhaps.'

'The ladies' retiring room,' she said faintly. 'If you could escort me there, I am sure I will be fine.' She raised a limp hand and pointed down a corridor that the servants had not bothered to light.

'Are you sure?' he asked, confused. 'I would have thought…upstairs, perhaps…'

'I have been here before,' she assured him. 'I know the way.'

He did not question further, but shepherded her in the direction she had suggested, towards the perfect spot.

When they drew abreast of it, she reached across his body and gripped the handle, turning it and giving a sharp, sudden tug to open the door beside him. At the same time, she staggered into him, pushing him off balance and through the darkened opening.

He had time for one brief, surprised curse as he realised what was happening. Then he grabbed her by the shoulder and carried her body along with his. They lurched together over the threshold, as the door slammed shut behind them.

Chapter Seven

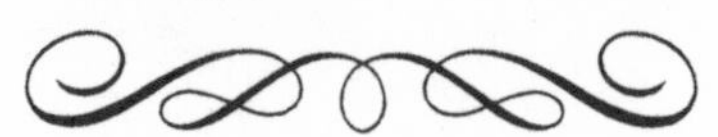

It had been a grave miscalculation.

Amy had had a vague recollection of the Middleton house, from previous visits. The door she'd thought she was choosing opened on to a small card room. It was well away from the rest of the house, but hardly uncomfortable.

Perhaps she should have turned right instead of left. The door she'd actually opened was for a cupboard. Now she was wedged chest to breast with Benjamin Lovell, in a space that was never meant to hold one person, much less two.

There was a moment of silence in the darkness punctuated by the sounds of their laboured breathing. Then he said in a low voice, so near to her ear that she could feel his breath moving her hair, 'Why, Miss Summoner, I had no idea you cared.'

Her own breath hissed out between her teeth as she stifled a dozen possible responses, all of them caustic. But it was her fault that they were here. It would only make things worse to snap at him.

Carefully, she fumbled for the door handle behind her, preparing to back out into the hall. Then, if possible, she would find a way to pretend this never happened. Her fingers closed not on metal but on his hand, which was wrapped around the handle and holding the door shut. She jerked her hand away. Even through her gloves, the nearness of his skin was dangerously exciting.

Amy unclenched her jaw, forcing herself to breathe slowly through her nose instead of her mouth. That did no good at all, for it flooded her senses with the intoxicating scent of the man beside her. She had not noticed his cologne when they had been in public, for it was subtle. Now she was drifting on a cloud of lime and laurel that was as soothing as it was intriguing.

She took another breath, through her mouth this time, and did her best to ignore it. 'Do not flatter yourself, Mr Lovell. You know my reason for trapping us here.'

'Really, I have no idea,' he said in a dry voice. 'Enlighten me.'

There was nothing to do but be honest. 'I did not wish you to sit beside Belle. The place was saved for someone else.'

'And rather than allow her to tell me so, you took it upon yourself to lock me in a closet,' he said, making her plan sound all the more illogical.

'We are both in the closet,' she reminded him. 'And the door is not locked.'

Behind her, the door rattled but did not open. 'On the contrary.'

'It cannot be,' she whispered, praying that he was wrong.

'Why not? That was the fate you planned for me, I'm sure. You planned to lock me in here. Then I would have to hammer on the door, interrupting a performance and embarrassing myself in front of my friends, all because you did not wish me to sit next to your sister.'

'I did not intend…' It was a lie. That was exactly what she had meant to have happen. Even if the man was a puffed-up bounder, she should have found a way to put him off that did not involve his total humiliation.

'I'm sorry,' she said at last. 'Not that it will do any good in the current situation.'

He sighed. 'Too true. I suppose we will both have to call for help. If we are loud enough, they will hear us over that canary they have screeching in the main room. Someone will come and open the door. It will cause the devil of a scandal when they find us together. But I am afraid it cannot be helped.'

'Please, do not.' She raised a hand to cover his mouth. This was far worse than letting him speak to Belle. What had she been thinking to allow herself to be trapped by him?

He took advantage of the opportunity to nip her fingers. Rather than painful, the pressure of his teeth through the white kid leather was shockingly pleasant. Hurriedly, she pulled her hand away again. 'Stop that.'

'Do not do this. Do not do that.' He tsked. 'Did you not wish to ruin my chances with Arabella? Being caught playing hunt the squirrel with her sister would most assuredly do so.' In the darkness, she imagined his mocking smile.

'I did not mean to do it by ruining myself as well.'

'Are you sure? If you wish to trap a husband, there is no quicker way to do it than to force him into such a compromising position.' The hand that had been holding her arm was stroking the bare skin between sleeve and glove. Suddenly, she felt as light-headed as she had pretended to be a few moments ago.

'For the last time, I do not wish to wed anyone. Most especially not you.'

'Then perhaps this is the sort of dishonourable liaison you spoke of on Bond Street. Maybe I am the one in need of rescue,' he said, his voice hoarse. 'It would be better for both of us if we were discovered immediately.' His hand stroked down her arm until her glove pooled at her wrist. Then he continued to her fingertips to pull it away, leaving her hand bare.

'What are you doing?' she whispered, though she was sure she knew. Even worse, she did not mind.

'Taking a forfeit,' he said, raising her hand to his lips again. 'You might think it amusing to play childish tricks with me, Amelia. But I am not some green boy put on this earth to be the butt of your joke. If you play games with a man, you must prepare for what will happen when you lose.'

He was right. It had been foolish of her to push this man to the point of anger. Even more foolish to become trapped with him in a situation that could lead to ruin for both of them. Suddenly, she was all too aware of the size of him and the feel of his body, hard against hers. She should at least have the sense to be frightened. Instead, she held her breath, eager to know what came next.

He pressed his mouth to her palm and she felt the tip of his tongue following the lines on her skin. She had once been to a gypsy who claimed to read one's future there. It had been nonsense, of course. The old woman had proclaimed her destined to a long and lasting love based on an unbroken wrinkle of skin.

But now, Mr Lovell was running his tongue along that very line, his lips creating a gentle suction. His teeth were teasing the flesh that the fortune teller had called the mound of Venus. She had hinted at a carnality that Amy and her school friends could not understand, though they had giggled over it at the time.

But today, she was sure she knew what had been meant. The pressure of those straight white teeth made her bite her own lip to keep from crying out.

She should do the sensible thing and pull her hand away, with some cutting remark about his unwilling attention. But she made no effort to move. It must be shock. Nothing more than that. She should not be enjoying this.

He took her inaction as permission to take more liberties. His other hand came up to cradle hers to his mouth and he bit down hard enough to make her jump. Then he turned it slightly, settling his lips over the web of skin between thumb and forefinger.

She gasped and yanked her hand away. 'What was the meaning of that?'

'I should think the meaning plain enough,' he said, in a voice that was annoyingly calm. 'As long as we are trapped in a cupboard together, we might as well find a pleasant way to pass the time.'

'You flatter yourself if you think I am enjoying this,' she said, though her breath came in gasps that proclaimed she lied.

'Then I must be doing it wrong.' The hand that had been on the door handle was now cupping her bottom. 'Is this better?'

Infinitely so. But Lord knew what would happen if she admitted the truth. 'If you need a woman to correct your technique, there are houses full of them in Covent Garden. I suggest you go there and leave proper young ladies alone.'

'I am not normally prone to such assignations. I certainly do not indulge in them at public gatherings. I am very conscious of my reputation.' He sounded puzzled by the statement, as though he needed to make the sort of maidenly assertion she could not think to make. 'Apparently, I'm more conscious of my rep than you are of yours.' This was followed with a pinch that made her jump forward, pressing herself even tighter to his body.

'I know perfectly well that this is improper,' she said. She put her hands flat on his chest, meaning to push him away. Instead, the fingers of her ungloved hand found the opening of his shirt, dragging a nail along the bare skin. 'It was never my intention to be in here with you.'

He sighed. 'I suppose that is as close as I will get to an apology. You must give over these attempts to separate me from your sister. I will meet her eventually, you know. And speak to your father as well.' Their lips were separated by a bare whisper of air. She could feel the imminent kiss, like the flutter of a moth's wing against her face.

'I only mean to forestall you until a worthy gentleman makes his move,' she reminded him. Perhaps, once he knew he had lost, things might be different between them. Or perhaps they would change right now. She opened her mouth, ready to yield.

But no kiss came. 'A worthy gentleman?' The air around him seemed to chill with a dangerous silence. 'What, exactly, is it about me that you find objectionable? Is it my character? I make sure that it is exemplary. Is it my birth? Because that does not seem to bother the rest of London.'

It was because she had thought him cold and demanding, when she'd overheard him at Almack's. He had been anything but cold, a moment ago. And under certain circumstances, demanding could be quite nice. 'It is more than that,' she said, searching for an explanation that did not insult. 'A match between you would be disastrous for all concerned.'

'You mean it would be a disaster for you,' he said. 'Since you are so free with your opinions of my character, let me enlighten you as to yours. When she marries, you intend to hang on your sister's skirts and burrow into whatever home she makes like a tick on a dog's back. Since you know I will not allow it, you cannot abide me.'

He thought of her as a parasite on her sister's happiness? And just now, she had been ready to… 'How dare you.'

'How dare I?' he said in a tone of mock outrage. 'With complete confidence, Miss Summoner. It is the common view of society that you are nothing more than a frustrated spinster. You had a horrible Season and no man would have you. Now you mean to spoil your sister's come out as well.'

'I am not frustrated,' she retorted, before she

could stop herself. She owed this man no explanation. 'My Season was not horrible.' It had been a sometimes delightful lesson in what men expected from women. She had survived it informed but unscathed. But her sister had a desirable body, a docile temperament and no understanding of the consequences of flirtation. If they were not very careful, she would not be so lucky. 'And Belle should not be out at all.' She bit her lip, for she was dangerously close to speaking the truth.

'Jealousy,' he said, satisfied.

'I am not jealous.' At least, she hoped she wasn't. It was not as if she had sought out Ben Lovell's attention. But why did life seem so much more exciting when she had it, and so disappointing now that she knew what he really thought?

'That is a shame.' He rested a finger on her cheek like a Judas kiss. 'If it is not that, then I must assume that, based on what you have heard of my past, your problem is nothing more than snobbery. In my opinion, pride is an even greater sin than envy.'

'You are too quick to assume the worst in me, Mr Lovell. It is not conceit that keeps me from helping you. It is that…' How could she explain without ruining her sister's chances with another? 'Belle is a special.'

'And I am not,' he finished for her, wilfully misunderstanding. 'You think I am all right for a tussle in the dark, of course. But not good enough to marry your sister.'

'We are not…tussling,' she said. Not yet, at least.

'Well, let me inform you of the truth, Miss Amelia, since you are so quick to assume you understand me. Despite what people might think, my birth was as legitimate as yours. Perhaps my pedigree would not be to your liking. But I have come far in life and mean to go further still. I will do it with or without the help of your family. At the very least…'

He reached behind her and she heard the click of a door handle that had apparently been unlocked all along. 'I have the sense to discover facts for myself and not assume the worst, just because I was told something by another. Good evening, Miss Summoner.'

And with that, he was gone, leaving her to retrieve her fallen glove and slink off to the retiring room to regain her composure.

Chapter Eight

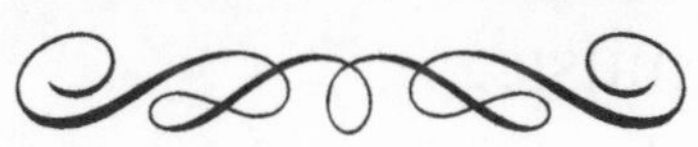

In the carriage on the way home, Ben stretched his feet in front of him, staring at the toes of his boots as Templeton yammered on about the evening from the seat opposite.

'Normally, I prefer lighter fare. A sprightly tune on a decent pianoforte. Something that one can hum the next day. But tonight's soloist wasn't half bad.'

Ben grunted in response. When he'd finally made his way to the music room, he had been too wrapped in his own thoughts to notice the entertainment.

'It is a shame you missed the first few songs. There was an absolute cracker with high notes that rattled the windows. It was in Italian, I think. I had no idea what she was saying. But still…'

He doubted Templeton had heard a word of what was sung, being far too preoccupied by the lovely lady at his side during the performance. From his seat in the last row, Ben had watched the pair of them, heads tipped towards each other, bobbing in time to the music.

The only saving grace of the evening was that there had been no repeat meeting with Amy Summoner. Miss Arabella had needed to depart immediately after the concert because Miss Amelia had taken ill at the beginning of the evening and stayed in the retiring room so as not to spoil her sister's enjoyment of the music.

Ha! When he'd heard the excuse, he'd wanted to shout to the whole room that, unless being green with envy was a debilitating condition, Amy Summoner was as right as the rest of them. She was simply hiding in the retiring room, waiting for the best time to reappear and ruin her sister's evening.

And his as well. His sole purpose in going to the event was to court the sweet and innocent Miss Belle. Instead, he'd spent the whole evening brooding over a woman who was as tempting as

Circe and twice as dangerous. What had he been thinking to shut himself up in a cupboard with her? He'd have been safer climbing into the tiger cage at the royal menagerie.

'Of course, if I had spent the evening making my own music, I doubt I'd have missed it.' He looked up to find Templeton staring at him with a knowing smile.

'What the devil are you talking about?' he said, daring the man to answer.

'You were absent from the room for several minutes after we arrived. I assumed it was because of a clandestine meeting with a member of the fair sex.'

'Do not talk rot.' Under his bluster, he felt the beginnings of panic. Who else had noticed his absence? What conclusions had been drawn?

Templeton took a deep breath. 'So the lingering scent of cologne I detect means nothing?'

Ben gave him what he hoped was a quelling glare. 'If you smell something, it is probably that bay concoction I picked up from Floris.'

Templeton gave another sniff. 'Definitely not. And it is not the lavender scent that Miss Arabella wears. I think what I smell is called Florida Water. Imported. Light, but exotic.'

Ben deepened his glare. 'Since when have you become an authority on ladies' colognes?'

Templeton raised his hands in denial. 'Not an authority, dear fellow. The scent is distinctive. Few wear it. In fact, only one woman I can think of.'

It was a warning then. If he walked about London reeking of Amy Summoner's cologne, no one would believe his sincerity in courting her sister. 'If you are speaking of Miss Amelia, she most likely spilled it on me during one of her many assaults upon my person.'

'I am sure that is it,' Templeton agreed with a smirk. 'But would it be such a bad thing if it were else? She is Lord Summoner's daughter and you are intent on marrying into the family. Your affections are not still fixed upon Miss Arabella, are they?'

'Have I given you reason to think otherwise?'

Templeton shook his head in amazement. 'I should think the fact that you have spent no time with the girl, in public or private, is an indication.'

'It is not for want of trying. Her perfume-spilling sister is doing her best to prevent it,' he said. 'Once I have got her out of the way, it is only a matter of time before I win Belle's favour.'

'I see.' If Templeton saw anything, his tone implied that what he saw was something quite different from Ben's vision of the future. 'As long as you are not wasting time with flirtation. It would reflect poorly on you if you were romancing one girl while seeking to marry another.' It would be even worse if the girls were sisters. Templeton did not have to say it for his meaning was plain.

'I know better than to do that,' he said, wishing it was true. Perhaps a peer could risk playing such dangerous games. But a man with no real rank and a dubious past might destroy his future trading kisses in closets.

Templeton nodded. 'Men have *known better* since Eve tempted Adam and the results are always the same.'

'Miss Amelia is not tempting me,' he insisted. At least, she was not trying to. As far as he could tell, his response to her presence was his own fault. 'And she is not fascinated by me as you suggested at first. She loathes me.' If she hadn't before, she most certainly did after he called her a frustrated spinster.

'That is a shame,' Templeton said, with a sympathetic nod. 'The pair of you seem to be very well suited.'

Ben laughed. 'She is proud, obstinate, domineering and far too clever for her own good.'

The silence in response implied that he had proved his friend's point.

'It does not matter what you think,' Ben said, ignoring the insult. 'My plans have not changed, nor has my opinion of Amy Summoner. She is a curse upon humanity.' Though she'd shown every sign of wanting to dally with him in private, she did not think him good enough for anything more than that. He'd had a lifetime's bitter experience with women who adored in the dark what they would not acknowledge in daylight. He did not need more of it from her.

More importantly, he did not need to tell her any more secrets. He could not even blame the hypnotic effect of her eyes. She had goaded him to revelation with a few choice words. 'No,' he said firmly. 'I want no part of Amy. But Belle Summoner is a different matter entirely.'

'She is, indeed, very different,' Templeton agreed. 'And yet, the pair of them are inseparable. Have you decided where Miss Amelia will sleep when she moves into your home after the marriage? As I recall, there is a blue bedroom at the end of the hall with a lovely view of the garden.'

And there was a cupboard for linens just around the corner from it. At the thought, Ben could feel the tips of his ears flushing pink with embarrassment. 'She will be in her own home, with her own husband by then.' Even if he did not succumb to another mad impulse and kiss her, the brief interlude they'd already shared would make his life hell.

'You have plans for her future?' Templeton leaned forward, surprised.

Unbidden, his mind returned to the brief encounter in the cupboard and the feel of her hand against his mouth. How would her lips have tasted? Would she have even wanted him had they been discovered and scandal forced their hand?

And what would happen between them if another opportunity for privacy presented itself?

And none of that had been what Templeton had meant by plans. 'She will be married before her sister,' Ben said, vowing that it would be true. 'I do not know to whom. But I will find the man and make the match if I have to drive them to Gretna myself.'

Then, perhaps, he could have some peace. Amy Summoner was, by turns, irritating, intriguing and enchanting. It was unnatural that such a woman should be alone. For her sake, and the preservation of his sanity, a match must be made.

Now they were home and getting ready for bed, it should be possible to relax. Although Amy had seen very little of it, tonight had been a success. Belle had spent the whole evening with Mr Templeton. Ben Lovell had been thwarted yet again in his desire to meet with her.

But she must be more careful in the future. After the few minutes spent with Mr Lovell, her nerves had been frayed to the point where she had been ready to forfeit her own reputation. It was fortunate that he had taken her dismissal of his suit so personally. Because they had begun talking about Belle, he had left angry and far sooner than he might have.

But when it had been just the two of them, alone in the dark and talking of nothing, things had been moving quickly towards a point where they would not have been talking at all. The feel of his kiss on her hand and his touch on her body would be her companions in bed for many nights to come.

Perhaps, when Belle was properly married to Mr Templeton, Ben Lovell might notice that there were other women worthy of his attention. There might even be one in the family he sought to join.

And if pigs flew it would not make them birds. Delightful as it was to be alone with him, she would never be anything more than his second choice. If she decided to marry at all, it should be to a man who loved her above all others. But feelings might change, with time. And it was not as if Ben Lovell had ever really loved Belle.

Then the familiar feelings of guilt rushed in to settle the matter for her. She should not even consider the possibility of her own marriage until she was sure that Belle's future was assured. There were some things more important than personal happiness. Married or unmarried, her sister was unable to manage without help and it was Amy's responsibility to care for her.

'Did you enjoy the music tonight?' Amy set aside the handful of pins she'd removed from Belle's hair and reached for the comb, dragging it through her blonde curls.

'It was pretty,' Belle said, smiling at her in the mirror.

Amy smiled back and uttered a silent prayer that the risk she had taken was not in vain. 'Did you enjoy the company?'

Her sister's face went blank.

'Did you like sitting next to Mr Templeton?' Amy said.

'He said I should call him Guy.'

This was progress. 'What did you say to him?'

'I told him he had a funny name.'

Amy winced. 'And what did he say to that?'

'He said it was a funny name. And he said my name meant pretty.'

This was much more encouraging. 'He is calling you Belle, now?'

'That's my name,' her sister agreed, unaware that such familiarity had meaning.

'Did he say anything else?' Amy held her breath.

'We were listening to the singer.' Belle gave her an impatient look to remind her that a concert was no place for conversation.

'Of course.' It was probably too soon to hope for a proposal, but Amy could not help it. She did not know how many more meetings with Mr Lovell she could stand. The man was both unbearable and irresistible.

'Did you have a nice time with Ben?'

Amy fumbled the comb, nearly dropping it. 'What makes you think I was with Mr Lovell?'

'You were not with him,' Belle said, smiling in surprise that her sister could not understand a simple question. 'Guy said I was not to worry about you because you were with Ben.'

'Of course.' Mr Templeton had seen them in the hall. She must hope that no one else had.

'Who is Ben?' Belle fixed her with a bright-eyed stare.

'He is not who I thought he was,' Amy said absently. He might seem cold, but he was not without passion. He was ambitious, but if he meant to better the world, it was a virtue, not a vice. And he was not illegitimate. Had he ever claimed to be a duke's bastard, or did the world jump to a conclusion that he did not correct?

But if he was not Cottsmoor's son, then who was he?

Chapter Nine

To say that Ben did not like the hubbub of Vauxhall Gardens did not do justice to his feelings on the place. More accurately, he did not want to like it. It was enjoyable, in a plebeian sort of way. If he wished to be seen as the sensible sort of politician who could lead a nation, he suspected a pleasure garden should be beneath notice.

But somewhere beneath the polished façade he'd cultivated, the simple youth he had been before meeting Cassandra was near to fainting with excitement at the prospect of a visit. There was music and dancing. Madame Saqui walked on a wire far overhead as balloons rose and fireworks lit the night sky. Try as he might to be aloof and sophisticated, how could he resist?

It was also a place where pretty, young girls

wandered about, loosely chaperoned and eager to test boundaries that could not be breached under the watchful eye of Almack's patronesses. It was a perfect place to separate Arabella Summoner from her overprotective sister and persuade her that, despite what she might have heard about him, he was the answer to a maiden's prayers.

But, as usual, the younger of the two Summoner girls was eluding him and the elder was all too easy to find. As he moved through the crowd and conversed with friends and acquaintances, he asked discreet questions about Belle's location. It seemed everyone had seen her just a moment ago. He remained perpetually one step behind.

And each time he stopped to reconnoitre Amelia was there, smiling in triumph. He would not be surprised to find that she was herding her sister around the grounds specifically to keep them apart. Amy Summoner had far too much time to meddle in the business of others. She needed some occupation other than arranging her sister's life.

And after the interlude at the Middletons' house, he had an excellent suggestion for her. He closed his eyes for a moment, reminding himself that she was the last person in the world he dare dally with. She could ruin his future with a single word to her father. But closed eyes only reminded him of discovering her secrets by touch when they had been shut up together in the dark.

If it been anyone else in the world, he'd have allowed himself to explore the depths of this fascination. Like the boy who longed to see fireworks, there was a part of him that could not seem to resist her. And though she might be too ladylike to admit to it, she was as eager as he was to see where another meeting might lead them.

All the more reason that he should find her a husband. He opened his eyes again, keen to dispel the fantasy with cold, hard truth. She was far too volatile for his tastes. She took far too much pleasure in tormenting him. And judging by her comments about his insufficiency, she would destroy him as a matter of principal, should she find out the truth about his past.

But a woman so warm and vibrant should not remain single. It was not just a nuisance, it was a waste. He could not abide wastefulness. How hard could it be to change her future? Her wits were quick enough and she was not unattractive. In fact, it was her exotic beauty that had first attracted his attention. If others did not see it, then her family name should have been enough to attract suitors like flies to a honey pot.

And yet, she had none. If he applied masculine logic to the situation, she would be married in no time. He would likely win the favour of Lord Summoner for taking the girl off his hands. And once she belonged to another, maybe he could stop thinking about her and return his focus to the more agreeable of the two sisters.

It was simply a matter of finding the right candidate to partner her. He glanced around the crowd, searching for a match, and found one almost immediately. Stanton Haines was walking towards him, balancing a stack of paper-wrapped ham sandwiches in his folded arms.

Ben calculated silently. Haines had a new phaeton and matched bays and a coat cut by the finest Bond street tailors. His apartments in Jermyn Street were decorated in the height of fashion. His winters were spent at his family estate, which was at least equal to the Summoner home. Ben suspected he must have close to ten thousand a year and more to come upon the death of his father.

Best of all, he was still single and claimed to be looking for a wife. In Ben's opinion, if the search had gone on for several years, Haines was not looking hard enough. The man was clearly in need of help. He put on a welcoming smile and raised a hand in greeting. 'Haines, old fellow.'

'Lovell,' his friend responded with a smile. 'Care for a sandwich?'

'They are all yours?'

'There is hardly enough meat in them to make a decent meal. I thought to combine it and throw the bread to the ducks. But I could spare one.' He eyed Ben suspiciously. 'You always have a hungry look about you.'

If this was meant as a jibe at his ambition, Ben would let it pass. 'Why not share with a young lady instead? Surely there is one here who would be better company than a duck.'

At this, Haines laughed and Ben put a guiding hand on his shoulder, pushing gently in the direction of the prey. 'You are already acquainted with Miss Summoner, I suppose.'

The other man's eyes took on the glazed expression that Ben often saw when conversation was turning to Miss Arabella. 'I have not. She is dashed hard to meet, you know. Her family guards her like a princess in a tower.'

'Surely not,' Ben answered, deliberately misunderstanding. 'I was riding with her myself, just the other day.' He paused, waiting for the good-natured ribbing that would follow had Haines been aware of his very public fall in the mud, but it did not come.

Instead, he said, 'You rode with her?' There was a proper amount of awe in his companion's voice at the achievement.

'I will introduce you, if you like.' He added a generous smile. 'Perhaps she would like a sandwich.'

'Yes. By all means, let us see if she is peckish.' Now Haines was not so much being led as pulling in his harness, eager to go forward.

Ben shepherded him towards the pavilion where he had last seen Amelia. 'There she is now. Miss

Summoner,' he called out, and the girl turned slowly to face him.

'Damn.' The legs of the man next to him locked and he dug in his heels like a stubborn mule. 'I thought you meant… Damn.'

But it was too late for him to change direction without being unspeakably rude. Ben pressed on, forcing the man the last few feet. 'Miss Summoner, how nice to see you again. Are you enjoying your evening?'

'Mr Lovell,' she said. The knowing smile she directed to him suddenly disappeared. 'I had been enjoying it.' The words left the clear implication that her pleasure had come to a sudden end upon seeing his companion.

'Have you met my friend, Mr Haines?'

'Yes.' If her greeting to him had been chilly, her acknowledgement of the other man was positively glacial.

'Miss Summoner,' Haines answered, with a shallow bow, never taking his eyes from hers, like a man facing down a wild animal.

'Mr Haines was wondering if you would care for refreshment.' He jabbed a sharp elbow in the other man's ribs, causing him to drop the top sandwich from the stack.

She looked down at it as if it was poison, then back up to stare at the two of them. 'No, thank you.'

'Well, then,' Haines said, with a sudden, relieved smile. 'I must go and ask someone else.' He shook Ben's hand from his shoulder, turned and left the two of them to an awkward silence.

She was staring at him now, and Ben wondered if it was her basilisk gaze that had put Haines off his game. Guy Templeton had claimed to be disturbed by it as well. Though it was threatening, he could not see what they found so troubling in it. Perhaps they felt the same desire he did, to stare back and study her as closely as she seemed to be studying him.

It was rude to stare, he reminded himself. And after their last meeting, showing this woman any interest at all sent a message he did not want to give. He did his best to change the stare into a surprised blink. 'Well, that did not go as well as I'd hoped.'

She responded with a raised eyebrow. 'What, precisely, were you hoping for, Mr Lovell?'

'Merely to broaden your acquaintance. I think it is a shame that such a pretty girl should have so few male friends.'

'Suitors, you mean,' she said, still not smiling. 'Perhaps no one wants to spend time with a frustrated spinster.'

There was no point in pretending their last meeting had not happened, if she meant to throw his hasty words back in his face. 'I apologise. I should not have said such a thing.'

'Even if it is true?' she said, finishing his thought. 'As I told you before, it is not.'

'But it surprises me that your sister receives so much attention, while you receive none at all.'

Instead of drawing her into a wistful admission of disappointment, she laughed. 'Do you talk this way to all the girls, Mr Lovell? You truly are new to the marriage mart, to say such things.' She added a coquettish flutter of her fan, as if to cement her disguise as just another silly girl.

He knew her too well for it to work. Her actions were as calculated as his were. 'I was merely matching my statement to your behaviour, Miss Summoner. You are a surprisingly blunt young woman.'

She nodded. 'Then let me use that candour to enlighten you. First of all, I am not moved by your obvious flattery. I will not apply false modesty and deny that I am passably pretty. But neither will I pretend that Belle is not my superior. I might be pretty, Mr Lovell, but my younger sister is a goddess.'

It was true. And said without a trace of the envy he expected to hear in such a statement. 'But some men do not want to worship at the feet of perfection. A goddess can be haughty and distant, not the warm flesh-and-blood woman who makes for a good…helpmeet.' What was he saying? He had been about to suggest something totally inappropriate for a conversation with a lady. Even worse, he had forgotten his purpose in talking to her was to gain the hand of that same goddess he was now denying.

If she had noticed the pause, she did not acknowledge it. 'If you knew Belle, you would discover that she is not the least bit distant. She is as human as the rest of us and as sweet tempered a creature as God ever put on this earth.' She gave him another arch look. 'That is why we are so careful in her company. I would not see her taken advantage of.'

'Of course not,' he agreed hurriedly. 'But though concern for your sister is admirable, it is a shame that she overshadows you.'

'I do not find it so,' she said. 'Because it is not true. Last night you assumed my Season was a failure. But you were not in London for my come out, Mr Lovell. I assure you, I received more than enough attention. In fact, I entertained the suit of your Mr Haines for several weeks.'

'You knew him?' By Haines's shocked reaction, it had been obvious that he knew of her. But Ben had assumed that it had been the same mock-shuddering response Templeton had given him and not based on actual familiarity.

Then he noticed the glint of nostalgia in her eye.

'What did you do to the poor fellow?'

'No more than he deserved.' The glimmer had become a twinkle of amusement.

'Let me be the judge of that. What did you do to him?'

'Would it not be better to ask what he did to me?' she said, now smiling with evil glee.

'Probably not. I did nothing at all to you at Almack's. We had not even been introduced. Your assault on me was unprovoked.'

The look in response to that was pointed and the fleck in her eye no longer seemed to dance. It glowed amber with accusation. 'You did nothing? Think again, sir.'

Had he done something to upset her? She seemed to think so. But what could it have been? He could not remember even hearing her name before the moment she dumped her lemonade on him. 'We were not speaking of me,' he said cautiously. 'But if you insist on it, I will ask the question in a way that is most likely to get me an answer. What did Haines do to you that caused you to respond in a way that left him so wary of you?'

She nodded in approval, as though he were a particularly smart pupil and she the tutor. 'I made my come out two years ago and he was one of the more promising suitors.'

'You had more than one?' It was rude of him to doubt the fact. Had he not just acclaimed her exceptionally pretty?

She responded with the sort of coy pout he'd have expected on any of the playful misses flirting by the pavilion. 'More than two, as well. I will make you a list, if you wish. It will save us both the trouble of you making introductions to people I already know all too well.'

'That will not be necessary,' he said, suddenly afraid to ask how many men had tried and failed to win her.

'But as I said, at one time, Mr Haines was a favourite.'

'Of yours?'

'Simply a favourite. But on an evening much like this, he lured me to the dark walks and attempted to take liberties.'

'He tried to kiss you.' This was quite at odds with the awkward spinster he had been imagining.

She gave him a disappointed look. 'You tried

to kiss me, Mr Lovell. Mr Haines tried to take liberties,' she repeated in a flat tone that made it quite clear she set her bounds of personal propriety well past a simple peck upon the cheek.

He was not sure if he was horrified or impressed. 'And I assume you were discovered. Was there was a scandal?'

She laughed. 'No on both counts. You should know that after our rendezvous at the Middletons' I have no intention of being forced by scandal to marry a man I do not respect.'

He was not sure which stung worse, her glib dismissal of their last meeting or the slight on his character. Did the woman have no heart at all? Then he remembered that it did not matter if she cared for him. She was not the woman he wanted.

She snapped her fingers in his face. 'Really, Mr Lovell, contain yourself. You are gaping at me like a beached cod.'

He gave a brief shake of his head to regain his senses. 'I apologise, Miss Summoner. I was shocked because I thought, for a moment, I was speaking with a normal young lady. Do go on.'

There was a brief flash of those exceptional

eyes to tell him that his answering shot had struck home. Then she continued. 'As I was saying, I had no desire to marry Mr Haines and he had no desire to explain to all of London that the bruise he received did not come from Gentleman Jackson.' She laid a finger on her cheek beside her nose.

'You blacked his eye?' His shock changed to awe. 'I should consider myself lucky to have escaped from the cupboard unscathed.'

'You only kissed my hand,' she said.

But what a kiss it had been…

'And a simple *no* did not dissuade Mr Haines,' she continued. 'He was most ardent. Should he claim to you that I broke his heart, it is an exaggeration. His feelings were no more engaged than mine were.'

At this, he hardly knew what to think. 'Were you in the habit of trifling with men's affections, Miss Summoner?'

She gave another flutter of her fan. 'Some mutual trifling might have occurred. I was poorly chaperoned and had no mother to warn me against flirting. Since my father left me to the care of servants when Mother passed, it was most foolish of him to think he could reappear when I was old enough to marry and put strictures on my behaviour.' While he saw no bitterness in her when she spoke of her sister, her feelings for her father were far more readable. At the mention of him, her lips thinned, her jaw tightened and the spark in her eye went so dark as to almost disappear.

'He was fortunate that you did not ruin yourself to spite him,' Ben said.

'Perhaps so. But that was long ago, Mr Lovell, and no real harm was done.' Mischief returned to the eyes peering at him from over her fan. 'Now, I am older and wiser and have charged myself to be sure no one takes similar advantage of my sister.'

Was it meant as a warning? It certainly seemed so. 'Once again, I assure you, Miss Summoner, that my intentions in that direction are nothing but honourable.'

'Honourable?' She lowered her fan to show there would be no dissembling between them. 'At Almack's, I heard you give high praise to my father and hardly a word for my sister. You had decided, since she was the prize of the Season, she would increase your stature. If that is all you care for, then you are not worthy of her.'

And that explained the lemonade. 'You should not have eavesdropped,' he said, though it was far too late to scold her on it.

'And you should not have said things you didn't want heard.' The fan returned and there was another flutter. 'It does not speak well of your judgement, Mr Lovell. Nor does it make you a suitable husband for Belle.'

Amy's opinion of him had been ruined before he'd even gained an introduction. But that did not mean his plans were hopeless. 'You should let Miss Arabella be the judge of her own heart.'

'Or my father?' The fluttering stopped again. 'Because my father is the person you really wish to please, is it not, Mr Lovell? Since he left the raising of Belle to me, it should not surprise you that I claim the right to approve her husband. I have been both mother and sister to her for the whole of her life.'

He had been wrong about her from their first meeting, flattering himself that she pined for him or assuming that she needed help to correct her character and find a husband. She was totally in control of her heart and her future and had set both aside for the sake of her sister. And from the first moment they'd met, his behaviour had been a textbook example of what not to do to gain her approval.

He held his hands up in a gesture of surrender. 'I have no choice but to apologise again for my behaviour. You are correct. It was reprehensible. I should not have spoken of my plans regarding a lady, especially not in a public place. But I hold firm in my belief that I would make a fine husband for your sister, despite what you might think of me. No man is perfect, Miss Summoner.'

She lowered her fan and studied him carefully, as if trying to decide whether to change her opinion. Then she shook her head. 'I am not seeking a perfect man for Belle, Mr Lovell. I am seeking one with the correct set of flaws.'

The conversation grew more curious the longer it continued. 'Tell me what you seek that I may mould myself into that man.'

Her eyes widened in surprise. 'Your character sounds exceedingly malleable.'

And once again, he was nagged by the desire for confession that sometimes took hold of him as he looked into her eyes. Did she really deserve to know just how changeable he was? He shook off the urge. 'Any man's character must be changeable for the better. But my heart remains constant.'

'Oh, I believe that, Mr Lovell. Your heart, if you have one at all, remains fixed on your own needs and desires. Since you have barely met Arabella, do not try to convince me that it is set on her.'

His needs and desires were synonymous with Arabella, since she was a means to an end. Put thus, even he could see how cold it was and how unworthy it would be in the protean eyes of the woman in front of him. Perhaps it was the straightest path to gain the power and admiration he wanted. But was it the right way?

Easiest was not always best. He knew from experience that what seemed pleasant often came with a price. It was one thing if he suffered. But suppose Amelia was right and her sister's future would be better with someone else in it? At the very least, the situation deserved more thought than he had given it.

'Miss Summoner! Miss Summoner!' The stout older woman who had been with the girls in Bond Street was hurrying down the path towards them, a look of panic on her reddened features.

'Miss Watson?' Amelia turned to her, instantly alert.

'Miss Belle is missing.'

Chapter Ten

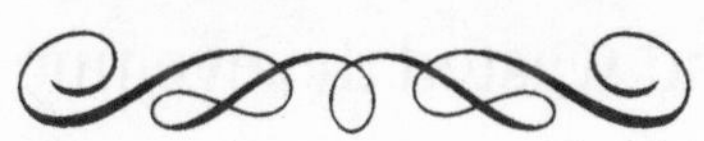

Belle was lost.

Amy struggled to take her next breath. It felt as if she'd been holding it for a lifetime. But that could not be. Everything had been normal, only a few seconds ago. Then, suddenly, her lungs had turned to iron and her throat had become a narrow glass tube that would shatter at the first gulp of air.

It had been her job to care for her sister. Her only, her most important job. And just as she had known some day she would, she had failed. Had Belle wandered away? Had someone taken her by force? Or had she been coerced?

It would take little more than a smile and the promise of a dance to lure her away from her chaperon. On a starry night, in a pleasure garden full of secret grottos and dark paths, anything might happen to her. Amy knew from experience that not all men who claimed to be were gentlemen and protected herself accordingly. But Belle was as innocent as a babe.

And Amy had wasted the evening sparring with Benjamin Lovell. It was a mere pretence that talking to the man had been about protecting her sister and not the pleasure she felt in a battle of wits. If she had truly been thinking of Belle, she'd have been at her sister's side and not indulging in distractions. Then she would not have disappeared.

What was she to do now? Miss Watson was frantic and she herself could barely manage to speak, much less to act. She turned to scan the crowd, eyes darting so fast between faces that she could not tell one from another. So many people and so many places to look. What was she to do?

'We must find her. Before…'

A hundred possibilities flashed through her mind, each more awful than the last. Before she could stop herself, a whimper of desperation escaped her lips.

'Really, Miss Summoner. We are in Vauxhall

Gardens, not Whitechapel. A few moments' absence is not the end of the world.'

'But Belle is my responsibility,' she whispered. 'If anything happens to her…'

Mr Lovell held up a hand. 'Say no more.' He turned to the chaperon, his voice calm but commanding. 'Where was she when last you saw her?'

'By the trained dogs.'

'And where have you been so far this evening? Was there any spot she was loathe to leave that she might have returned to alone?'

'She likes dancing,' Amy managed at last.

'Then, Miss…' Mr Lovell gave a pointed look to the chaperon.

'Watson,' Amy supplied.

'Then, Miss Watson, please return to the pavilion to check the dancers. If you do not find her there, proceed systematically towards the east. We will search west and enlist any friends we find along the way to help us. We will find her in no time, I am sure.'

His voice was like a soothing balm on Amy's nerves. On some level, she had always enjoyed the rumbling bass sound of it, as he had argued with her over every small thing. But now it was even and calm. With each word it loosened the grip of the panic that had taken her.

He reached out to take her arm. 'Come, Miss Summoner. Do not distress yourself. Let us locate your sister and set your mind at rest.'

For a moment, she hesitated. If she accepted his help and they found Belle in some unfortunate or compromising situation, would he use it to his advantage?

He sensed her misgivings and answered the question she hadn't asked. 'Let us worry over our previous conversation at a later time. For now, we must locate Miss Arabella. It is probably nothing, you know. In any case, I am the soul of discretion and you are in need of a friend.'

'Thank you.' She felt the last of her fear dissipate, replaced by confusion. She had always longed for a friend to share some of the burden of caring for Belle. But she'd never have thought such aid would come from Benjamin Lovell. Now he was leading her deeper into the park, stopping at each attraction to search the people assembled there.

'How old were you?'

'I beg your pardon?' He was looking ahead of them into the crowd and his question had seemed to come from nowhere.

'How old were you when your mother died?'

'Five,' she said, equally distant. She had been so small. But Belle had been even smaller. From the first moment she'd seen her, Amy had known that the tiny baby with the blue-tinged skin was in need of protection.

'Ten,' he muttered in response.

She tightened her hand on his arm, waiting for explanation.

'I was ten when my father died. Old enough to remember what it was like before I was forced to become man of the house.'

'I am sorry,' she said, in response to the familiar pain of loss she recognised in the words.

'But you were not much more than a babe yourself. Where was your father in all this?'

'At first, he was lost in grief for our mother. But when Parliament was in session he had the business of governance. We were too young to come to London for the Season. We were left in the country.'

'And you took it upon yourself to be sure that things ran properly while he was gone,' he finished. 'You cried yourself to sleep at night, didn't you? And woke each morning afraid to leave your bed, lest this be the day you failed in your mission and everything fell apart.'

'How did you know?' she whispered.

He answered with the sad smile of someone who had spoken from experience. 'I slept better after I went to live at Cottsmoor. In time, there were new things to disturb my dreams. But when I was removed from their cause, the old fears subsided.'

'Are you are suggesting that I let her go?' Amy said slowly. 'I do not know how.' Though she wanted to resist, the idea of gaining her own freedom was more seductive than any man had been.

'When she marries, you will have to,' he said.

But that had not been the plan. She was not going to abandon her sister. She just needed someone to share the duties. If there was a man she could talk honestly to, who understood Belle's difficulties and was clearheaded in crises, her life would be much easier. After talking to him tonight, it seemed that Benjamin Lovell might be just the husband she had been looking for.

The husband for Belle, she reminded herself. For a moment, she had lost sight of the goal altogether. Mr Lovell wanted to marry Belle and had just won her approval. But now that she had remembered it, why did the future feel so empty? Had she grown so used to defining her existence around the care of her sister that she could not imagine how to live life for herself?

Or was it because she took personal pleasure in leaning on Ben Lovell's arm as they searched the park? She did not wish to marry him or anyone else. He was not the first man who had flirted with her. Whispers in darkened cupboards meant nothing to either of them. And though admirable, his help and concern tonight was no more than she'd have expected from any honourable gentleman.

But in her heart, she wanted it to be more. It was likely proof that she was becoming the frustrated spinster he'd accused her of being. None of this mattered if Belle was lost. She must not be wasting energy speculating when there were more pressing matters to attend to. She scanned the crowd, searching for a familiar face. 'We have been to the acrobats, the supper rooms and down the colonnade, but no one has seen her. Where could she have gone?'

'I think it is time that we look in the areas that are not so well lighted,' he said, in an offhand manner.

It was exactly the place she most feared to find her sister. With their dim, winding pathways, the dark walks of Vauxhall were a notorious meeting place for young lovers. More than one gentleman had suggested the place to her during her first year out. Some had even succeeded in taking her there. But even then she had been far more worldly than Belle and knew when to call a halt to straying hands and lips.

She swallowed her dread. 'Let us go, then. Quickly.'

He patted the hand in the crook of his arm. 'Are you not afraid of what people will say, should they see us there together?'

'They will probably assume you are taking your life in your hands,' she snapped. 'But I do not care what they think, as long as they do not suspect the truth.'

Despite the seriousness of the situation, he chuckled. 'Take heart, Amelia. If you have the presence of mind to be sarcastic, things cannot be too dire.' Then he led her forward, out of the light.

It was just as she remembered it. The hundreds of lanterns that hung in the trees over the rest of the park became a distant glow that disappeared once they passed the first curve in the path. The only light remaining was the glimmer of moonlight filtered through the trees above them. They paused for a moment so that their eyes could adjust to the darkness. But now he was the one who hesitated and she was the one to tug his arm to lead him forward.

'A moment, please,' he said, still rooted to the spot, 'while I decide how best to go on.'

She snorted. 'You act as if you have never been here before.'

There was a profound silence from the man at her side.

'Really, sir? Do not tell me…'

'If one wishes to kiss a pretty girl, it is not necessary to drag her into the bushes,' he said, irritably.

'Nor is it necessary to drag her into a closet,' she replied.

'You instigated that encounter,' he reminded her. 'You have more experience here, as well. Do not try to claim I was a bad influence upon your character. From my standpoint, the opposite appears to be true.'

Before she could frame a retort, she heard her sister's voice, calling her name, far too loudly.

'Amy?' Belle appeared around the next bend in the path, smiling broadly and oblivious to the impropriety of discovering or being discovered.

'Shh.' Amy held a cautioning finger to her lips.

By her sister's puzzled expression, Amy was about to be peppered with loud questions about the need for silence.

Amy touched her lightly on the arm to reassure herself that all was well. 'The birds are asleep in the trees. We do not want to wake them.'

Belle nodded in agreement.

'Why did you leave Miss Watson?'

'It is easier to see the fireworks in the dark,' Belle replied.

There was more than a little logic to that. But agreeing with her would not get Belle to safety. 'It might be hard to see them through the trees. You will miss the balloon launch as well.'

Belle blinked. 'I would not want to miss that.'

'Perhaps I might be of assistance.' And now Mr Templeton was there, polite as always, offering his arm to Belle. 'May I escort you to the fireworks grounds, Miss Arabella?'

'That would be most helpful,' Amy supplied, not giving her sister a chance to refuse. Then she paused. When Templeton appeared, had he come from the lighted park behind them or from further up the dark path? She puzzled over it for only an instant before deciding that it was a matter that could be discussed at home, if it was discussed at all. 'But please, Belle, first you must go and find Miss Watson and tell her you are all right. She is at her wits' end.'

Belle looked distraught at the thought that she had caused trouble.

Mr Templeton gave her a brief, encouraging smile and then replied, 'We will find her this instant and set everything to rights. Come, Miss Summoner.' And then they were gone and Amy was alone in the dark walks of Vauxhall, with Benjamin Lovell.

For a moment, they stood silent, listening to the rustling of the wind in the leaves and the occasional whispers and sighs of couples alone in the dark. When she gathered the nerve to speak it was to state the obvious. 'Well, we have found her.'

'Safe and sound, just as I promised.' In the dim light, she could see his supremely confident smile.

Belle had not been alone. But it did not seem to bother him. 'Will you keep our secret?'

He touched her shoulder. 'I saw nothing out of the ordinary tonight.'

'Thank you. And thank you for your kind words as we walked.' Perhaps relief made her foolish. Perhaps it was the moonlight. Or perhaps it was simply that she wanted to do it. But before she could stop herself, she was up on her tiptoes and leaning forward to press a kiss on his cheek.

He responded without hesitation, turning his head so their lips met. There was an instant where she might have withdrawn, pretending shock where she felt none and ending the kiss. Instead, their mouths opened on one another's and their tongues tangled in a frenzied caress. It was everything she'd hoped it would be.

His hands took hers and lifted them, wrapping them around his neck. Then he clasped her around the waist and pulled her off the path, deeper into the undergrowth. Despite the darkness, the worry of a few moments before burned away like morning mist in the first rays of sunlight. She wanted to strip herself bare and bask in the heat of that sun until it had touched every part of her body.

His hand rose again to touch her cheek. Then it stroked down to grasp a breast and squeeze it possessively.

She whimpered with desire and writhed against him, eager to follow the moment where it led.

He answered with a shaky sigh. 'From the first moment we met, you have been a hazard to my peace of mind, Miss Summoner.'

'Amy,' she whispered back.

'Amy,' he said and touched her lips with his again.

'And do you value your peace?' she asked as he rained desperate kisses down her throat.

'I am learning to do without it,' he said. Then he pulled away, setting her gently back on her feet. 'But I had best not lose my common sense as well. If we are gone any longer, someone will miss us.'

She doubted the truth of that. When she had been younger and trying to shock, no one had noticed what scandal she was courting. Now, if she was gone, anyone who might care would assume she was doing some sensible thing that needed doing. No one would guess she was trading kisses in the dark with Ben Lovell. She sighed and straightened her gown. If she meant to lecture her sister on propriety, she had best not flout it herself. 'Very well. Take me back to the pavilion, Mr Lovell.'

She paused, waiting for the invitation to use his given name.

None came.

Chapter Eleven

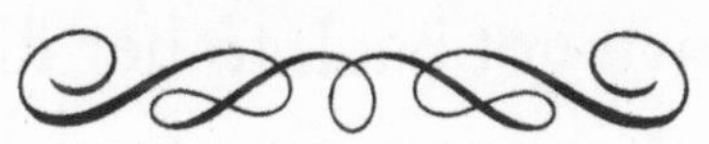

The next morning found Ben in the receiving room of the Summoner town house. Even though he was unobserved, he forced himself to stand at the window, facing the street as if admiring the view. Despite the purpose of the room, it was doubtful that Lord Summoner would come to him. More likely a footman would come to lead him to an office or study. In either case, he would not be caught pacing about the room like a caged animal. No hint of nervousness must spoil his first introduction with the one man in London he most wished to meet.

Assuming that it had not been spoiled all ready. The invitation had arrived with his first morning post, written by the great man himself and not some secretary or underling. But there was nothing in the brief note to indicate a purpose for the meeting.

So here he stood, resolutely still, trying not to focus on the most likely scenario. If someone had seen him leaving the dark walks with Amelia, word might have got back to her father. If so, he had been summoned to give an account of himself. Either he was about to be warned off or Summoner would expect him to make the offer that a gentleman should.

On reflection, he was surprised to realise that little pressure would be necessary to bring him to accounts. Though Templeton had suggested that one daughter was much like another, marrying Amelia had never been a secondary course of action, should he fail to attain the primary goal of Arabella's hand. Though his reasons for marrying were rational and analytical, it seemed too callous to swap sisters like cravats, when the first knot failed.

But now? When he thought of Amy, he was dangerously close to an involvement of the heart. Even worse, his body clamoured for a more intimate match and the sooner the better. When they were alone together, he was possessed by an earthy, primal attraction that he did not feel when looking at the ethereal Arabella.

Even now, when he should be in terror of the meeting about to occur, he could imagine torn and scattered clothing, and frenzied thrusts while staring down into passion-drugged, mis-matched eyes.

It was settled, then. Her father's permission, one simple question to the lady, three weeks to read the banns and he could begin acting on that passion with vigour and frequency.

At the thought, he reached for a handkerchief to mop a drop of cold sweat from his brow. He had but to look at his own past to remember why one did not trust heart and groin to make important decisions. Though it all might end well, the path to success was lined with tumult and heartache. Ranked in a lifetime of female acquaintance, Amy Summoner scored a close second in the administration of pain and suffering.

It had taken years for Cassandra to break his heart. Last night, after one kiss from Amy, he'd been ready to let it shatter all over again. If he took her to bed, it would be the death of reason and free will.

But what a glorious, hero's death it would be. Despite what one promised at the altar, it was not really necessary to love when one married. He respected her and he wanted her. That was more than enough. He would give anything else she required of him, but he would keep possession of his heart.

A footman interrupted his thoughts and led him down a long hall. It ended in a heavy oak door that stood open, ready to receive him. He passed through it to find Lord Geoffrey Summoner seated at an enormous desk in front of the window. He was sifting through the stack of letters before him, deliberately oblivious to the man he had invited for a meeting.

Ben refused to let himself be fazed by it. Instead, he stood before the desk, waiting patiently to be acknowledged.

After a few seconds, he looked up and Ben bowed. 'Lord Summoner.'

Summoner responded with a smile that was both warm and genuine, as if he had actually been looking forward to the visit. 'Mr Lovell. Please, sit down.'

He indicated the chair before the desk and Ben

sat. 'How good to see you. Does the day find you well?'

'Indeed, my lord.'

Summoner steepled his fingers. 'And I suppose you are wondering at the purpose for the meeting.'

Ben gave a brief nod and smiled back at him. 'If there is something you require of me I am at your service.'

'Require of you…' Summoner smiled again, drumming his fingers against each other as if he had a surprise that he was not ready to reveal. 'I am merely interested in seeing if you are half the man my friends seem to think you. At White's they speak well of you.'

'I am glad to hear it, my lord.' He was far more than glad if it meant that his indiscretion with Amy had not been discovered.

'You are thought to be moderate in all things, intelligent, well spoken and wealthy enough to be your own master.'

Ben gave another nod of modest acknowledgement.

'And you are in search of a wife,' Summoner finished.

Ben blinked in surprise and prepared to revise his previous assumption, then gave another, hesitant nod.

Summoner cleared his throat. 'I have a daughter…' He paused. 'Two daughters, actually. Both unmarried.'

Ben blinked again. There was still no indication of censure in the man's tone that might hint at knowledge of how well he already knew Amy. Instead, it sounded rather like Summoner meant to arrange a match himself. Finally, he nodded. 'I have met them both. They are lovely girls and do you credit, my lord.'

Summoner let out a relieved breath. 'Thank you, Mr Lovell. It does a father's heart good to know they are admired. But as I said earlier, I want to see one of them in particular settled with a man I can respect.' He gave Ben a long appraising look. 'Everyone I know speaks well of you. You have the means to care for her and the ambition to make a bright future from what you have already been given.'

Fraud. Upstart.

Ben silenced his doubts and responded as a man

of his position would be expected to. 'That is my goal, sir.'

'Then I see no reason why we shall not both have what we wish.'

At this, Ben blinked twice. Of all the scenarios he had imagined for his future with the Summoner family, being approached by the father and solicited to court the daughter was not one of them. Was the man really so doubtful as to Amy's chances of success that he was willing to barter her away? 'Your blessing on my suit sets my mind at rest,' Ben said cautiously.

'On your suit?' Summoner gave a short laugh. 'You have my consent to a marriage, Mr Lovell.'

Even though it had been his plan to ally with the family through marriage, things were moving too fast for comfort. 'I have not yet spoken to the lady on the matter,' Ben reminded him. 'There is no guarantee that she will have me.' It was far more likely that she would hand him his head for settling matters with her father before proposing.

Summoner gave a dismissive wave of his hand. 'When you do, you will find her in agreement. Young girls are far too flighty to make such decisions based on their hearts. And she truly is the most obedient of children. When I tell her that you are my choice, she will agree without argument.'

For a moment, Ben could not manage to respond at all. It had been his plan to take only the first step. But it appeared that he had all but completed his journey to the altar. And after that—

The older man interrupted his reverie. 'There is also the matter of a settlement. As I understand it, you do not need my money. I have little land, other than the house in the country, which is entailed. But I control two seats in the House of Commons. They cannot very well be given to my girls.'

He paused to laugh at the idea of women in office. But Ben saw it for what it was: a carefully structured pause to build drama for the offer he was about to extend.

'You seem like a bright young fellow. Have you considered standing for office?'

Though he had seen it coming, it still took effort to hide his amazement. He had gone to bed dreaming of the future and woken to find his future was made. He answered with as much composure as he could manage, 'Indeed, my lord. It is my fondest wish to serve.'

Summoner nodded. 'A noble ambition, to be sure. Then we are in agreement. Welcome to the family, Mr Lovell.' The man stood and offered his hand.

Ben rose as well, giving it a firm shake. 'Thank you again, my lord. I will endeavour to exceed your expectations of me. And I will do my utmost to make your daughter as happy in the future as you have made me today.'

'Excellent.' Summoner stepped from behind the desk. 'I am so glad to have the matter settled and so early in the Season. Social events are tiresome for Belle and I had no wish to put her through more than was necessary to secure a match.'

'Belle?' Had they discussed the identity of the bride to be? Or had he just assumed he knew it?

'We call her that at home,' the other man said, misunderstanding his confusion. 'Arabella is a beautiful name, but so formal.'

'Of course,' Ben answered, his mind still racing to catch up.

'We call her elder sister Amy for the same

reason,' he said. 'Sometimes I worry that there is power in the names we give. Amelia always struck me as an excellent name for a spinster. And my Amy has grown adamant that she will never marry. Many men have tried, but there is no changing her mind.'

How many men? And just how hard had they tried to persuade her? It would be naïve of him to think that a woman with a passionate nature and the sense to be discreet would deny herself pleasure if it was offered. It was obvious, after their discussion last night, that he was not the first man to have kissed her. It was unlikely that he would be the last.

'You are certain she will never marry?'

'She's refused more than one offer,' Summoner assured him, 'and has been most adamantly opposed to men I've suggested for her. I suppose I should be thankful that she has not run off with a dancing master, or some such foolishness. If she means to spite me, remaining respectably unmarried pales in comparison to actively courting disgrace.'

Her devotion to her sister outweighed any desire to elope to spite her father. Once Belle had married, perhaps she would consider it. Or would she return to one of the suitors she had already rejected? In either case, Ben doubted she would want him once she knew he had Lord Summoner's approval. And if he truly did not want to involve his heart in his marriage, it might be wise to take the perfectly lovely daughter being offered to him and not the one who raised such conflicting and uncontrollable emotions in him. 'I have heard that Amelia intends to follow her sister to her husband's house,' he said, cautiously.

'Perhaps that is her intention,' Summoner replied. 'But I have no plan to indulge it and neither should you. My daughter can refuse to marry if she wishes, but it does not entitle her to live off her sister's husband under the guise of sisterly devotion.'

'I am glad to hear you say it, my lord.' If he meant to wed Belle, he could not be staring at those disquieting eyes and luscious lips for the rest of his married life. Even a wife who did not expect total fidelity from her husband would not stand for an affair inside the family. Nor did he want to give himself up to a woman who might be tempting him now, just to spite her father.

'And if I am honest, Belle is far too influenced by her sister,' Summoner said with a worried frown.

That might explain why she had been in need of rescue the previous evening. She had only followed the bad example of her sister. 'I am sure Miss Amelia regrets any harm she might have done,' he said. This, at least, was true. Amy had been genuinely distraught at her sister's absence and unwavering in her devotion.

'Once we have separated the pair of them, you must be Belle's guide in all things. It is your duty, as husband. I trust that you will have a care for her, sir. Simply have a care.' There was a slight tremor in the older man's voice that spoke of barely controlled emotion.

'Of course, I will care for her. With all my heart,' Ben added. Or some of his heart, at least. The poor man was feeling the loss of his daughter already. It could do no harm to hint at more affection than he felt for the girl. He would generate it easily enough, after he actually spent some time with Belle and they'd discussed the wedding between them without Amy or her father there to organise the matter for them.

'See that you do, my son.' Summoner paused again, his face becoming suddenly grave. 'After you leave this room, there will be no turning back from the matter.'

'I have no intention of it,' Ben assured him.

'No intention? That is hardly enough assurance for me. Men intend many things. But how many actually follow through?'

Was Summoner now having second thoughts? It did not matter. With the ultimate goal in sight, Ben would not allow himself to fail. 'I cannot speak for other men, Lord Summoner. But when I intend to do a thing, it is as good as done.' If he could tell the man just how far he had come on intention alone, he might actually be impressed. Then he would throw Ben from the house for being an upstart imposter.

'Would you be so kind as to swear to the matter?' Summoner turned away and walked to the nearest bookshelf. When he turned back, he was holding what appeared to be the family Bible. He set it down on the desk between them.

'Of course. But…' Was it truly necessary?

'I would not normally be so demanding. But Belle is…special.' There was the choke in his voice again, as if he could not bear to be parted from her.

Even so, if a man gave his word, an oath should not be required. But if a man's life was based on lies, then did he truly have honour to swear on? It was a question that he'd asked himself many times over the years. But today was not the day to search for the answer.

Summoner sensed his doubts and pushed the book towards him. 'Swear to me, that, from the time you leave this room until the end of your life, there will be no second thoughts and no regrets at your haste. Swear you will do nothing, no matter how small you might think it, to hurt my daughter.'

'As you wish,' Ben said and laid his hand down on the leather cover. 'I swear before God that I will care for your daughter and do only what is best for her.'

Summoner nodded. 'Very good.' He laid his hand down as well to cover Ben's. 'For I swear, if you break this oath, so shall I break you. You have a bright future in front of you, Boy. But if you hurt my child, embarrass her, disgrace her, or do anything to sully her reputation, there will not be a scrap of hope left in you, once I have finished with you.'

The threat was made with such conviction that Ben wanted to snatch his hand away in denial. But it did not matter what he wanted to do. It was already too late to change his mind. The man had said no retreat and he had promised.

Since the prize was Belle Summoner, it would not be a hard promise to keep, as long as he stayed far away from Amelia. And once she realised she was free of her responsibility for Belle, she would not be a spinster for long.

It would take a particularly brave man to stand up to both her strong will and her protective father. But he should not be brooding on it. That woman's future was no longer his concern. She could kiss as many men as she liked, in Vauxhall or a cupboard. Since she was not to be a member of his household, he need never know of it.

Considering how much the prospect of Amelia kissing other men annoyed him, the less he knew about it, the better.

Chapter Twelve

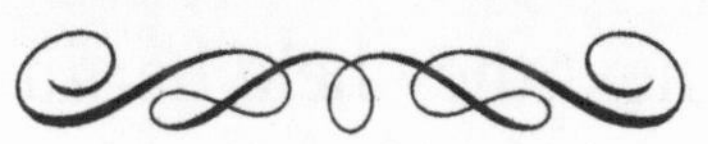

When Amy awoke the morning after Vauxhall, the sun was surprisingly bright and the sky an unusually clear shade of blue. Her breakfast chocolate was delicious as well. The song of the sparrows on her window sill was so delightful that she raised the sash and rewarded them with the last of the crumbs from her toast. Fortunately, she was too practical to mistake the reason for her euphoria.

Benjamin Lovell had kissed her.

It had been almost three years since the last time she'd been kissed. Was that long enough to forget how it had felt? She remembered those early kisses as awkward, wet and messy. When her beaus had felt confident enough to risk a caress, she had been more annoyed by it than aroused.

They always seemed to be holding her too tight, or not tightly enough.

And to a man, they had seemed to enjoy the whole thing more than she had. They'd sighed and moaned, and swore that they would not eat or sleep until next they held her in their arms.

In return, she'd felt nothing in particular. She had grown good at dissembling, for it hardly seemed polite to tell them she felt no matching ardour. If she was doing it wrong, she had no intention of admitting her ignorance. But in the end, she had come to the conclusion that when it came to love, men were actually the more flighty and fanciful of the sexes. To spare their masculine pride, women pretended to have the more sensitive feelings and the delicate and easily broken hearts. It certainly seemed that the men who courted her were genuinely disappointed when she refused their offers.

But what else could she do? She had found no real favourite amongst them and she did not think she could abide an entire life pretending to more than she felt for any of them. And there was always Belle and her future to consider.

Then she had kissed and been kissed by Benjamin Lovell. Had she been overly vulnerable because she was so used to handling all problems herself that she had forgotten what it was like to lean on anyone? Was it because he was a much more handsome rescuer than her previous suitors had been? Was it the masterful way he had come to her aid when Belle had disappeared, stunning her to reticence and taking control? For the first few minutes she could do little more than allow him to lead her about the park, searching crowds and questioning strangers. Sensing how frightened she was, he had teased her until she regained her nerve. Then, when they had found Belle in a compromising situation, he had sworn to keep her secret. She had needed a hero. And when she had turned to him, she'd found no sign of the unfeeling social climber she had overheard at Almack's.

Was it the combination of all those things that had made their need so immediate and mutual when, at last, they were alone together in the dark? As they had been in the cupboard at the musicale, his kisses had been so rapturous, his so touch possessive, her body had tingled, even in the places he was not kissing.

With other men, she'd always ended things before they got out of hand and demanded a return to the lights of the pavilion. But last night, if Mr Lovell had asked her to lay down in the grass and submit that instant, she'd have done it without a thought. She'd had to depend on his clear head to rescue her from disaster. He had been the perfect blend of gentleman and rogue. In the space of an hour, she was undone and happy to be so.

What was he thinking today? She doubted he was dancing around his rooms as she had done earlier and laughing over nothing. But she hoped that he was thinking of her and smiling as he did. Perhaps he was contemplating their next meeting. And maybe, just maybe, he was planning to call on her, to take her driving, or for a walk in Kensington Gardens.

She was infatuated. She had been so before, when she was a silly young girl. It would pass, in time, like a cold or a mild influenza. Passionate arousal was an unfamiliar and possibly new symptom. But as long as she did not explore any more dark, secluded spaces with him, she would survive it as well.

But suppose it was something more?

It was probably not. She did not have the time or the desire to fall in love. Nor had Mr Lovell given her reason to hope. He had not even offered the use of his first name. She absolutely refused to fall in love and allow her heart to be broken by his uninterest.

If anyone was going to fall in love first, it should be him. Then, if she felt so inclined, she would love him in return.

To that end, she dressed with exceptional care in her favourite morning gown of gold-striped muslin that suited the amber cross Father had given her on her last birthday. Admiring herself in the mirror, she'd never have claimed to be as beautiful as Belle. All the same, she looked exceptionally pretty this morning. One might even call her adorable. She had only to find her disciple to test the effect.

Even though she had prepared for company, she didn't actually expect it. The last person she expected to find when she descended the stairs to the ground floor was Mr Lovell, already standing in the hall with a puzzled expression on his face, staring down the hall towards her father's study.

'What are you doing here?' she demanded. There were no trace of society manners in the question. She stopped to remind herself that, even though he was used to her treating him with brusque uninterest, things had changed between them. As an afterthought, she softened her words with a smile and a toss of her head and prepared to start again.

'I just spoke with your father,' he said. The response was delivered in a monotone that proved his usual town bronze had abandoned him. Neither did he answer with the smile he'd worn last night, when they had parted.

'Is something the matter?' If Father had got wind of what had occurred at Vauxhall he might have summoned Ben to account for it. Since her father had done nothing about her previous trips into the dark walks, it was surprising that he should take an interest now.

'No,' Ben said slowly. 'Nothing is the matter. We have been discussing your sister's future.'

After what they had done last night, he had come to talk about Belle. Her mind flooded with responses, but the one she most wanted to give was the one pride would not let her say aloud.

How could you?

Instead, she answered in the distant tone she'd used with him when she was trying to put him off. 'Really? You obviously did not consult her in the matter, since she is still abed. What did you two men decide between you about Belle's life and happiness?'

'I am on my way to arrange for a licence,' he said, his voice still flat. 'The banns will be read for the first time this Sunday.'

'And at what point do you mean to speak to the bride?' she said, horrified. She had known his plan. Why did she think a few kisses would change it? 'And when you do, will you tell her what happened last night, after we found her?'

'Last night was a mistake,' he said. Though he stood a few feet from her, it was as if he was delivering a line in a play, speaking in her direction, but not to her. He looked at her, but not into her eyes.

'A mistake? Yes, I believe it was.' It was the biggest mistake she had made in years. The sort of error a green girl would make before she learned to protect her heart as carefully as her reputation. She had lost her head and kissed him, and encouraged him to kiss her in return. Then she'd allowed herself to believe that it might be more than a typical male response to her wanton behaviour. Now he was about to tell her that any further contact between them would be impossible, since he was going to marry Belle, just as he had meant to, all along.

She spoke before he could. 'Do not worry. My curiosity is satisfied. There was nothing about the experience that I wish to repeat.'

His gaze snapped to meet hers. She could see by the sudden flash of anger there that he wanted to insist that she was lying. The kiss had been phenomenal. It was the sort of passion that came along once in a lifetime. How dare she deny it?

Then he remembered that, for all their sakes, the kiss had to mean nothing. The light in his eyes died and he responded in the same unemotional voice. 'I am glad we are in agreement.'

'On that, perhaps,' she said. 'But my opinion of your marriage to my sister is the same as it ever was. You will not suit.'

He raised an eyebrow. Some of his original Almack's hauteur was returning. 'Lord Summoner approves of me and has sanctioned the match. You do not have a say in it.'

'The fact that you do not value my opinion makes it no less valid,' she said. 'You will know soon enough that I am right. Then perhaps you will find the decency to withdraw your offer.'

'Disabuse yourself of the notion, Miss Summoner,' he said, finally showing his annoyance. 'I gave my word that the wedding would go on, no matter what happens. Your father is happy with it, I am happy with it and your sister will be happy as well, because I promised that I would make her so.'

'If you are happy, then why are you shouting?' she asked triumphantly.

'I *am* happy! And I am not…' he lowered his voice and finished '…shouting.' He took a deep breath and returned to the impassive man whom she'd found at the bottom of the stairs. 'The only one not satisfied with the situation is you. But there is no pleasing a person who makes such a concerted effort to be contrary. Now, if you will excuse me? I have a marriage to arrange.' With that, he turned and left her.

She waited only a moment before turning down the hall in the opposite direction and hurrying to her father's office. She did not bother knocking or waiting for permission to enter, but barged into the room and threw herself into the chair in front of the desk.

'Amelia?' Her father looked up, not even trying to pretend that he was too busy to give her his full attention.

'What have you done?'

'If you are here, then you already know. I assume you spoke to Mr Lovell in the hall.'

'He said you sanctioned the match.'

'He is the perfect choice,' her father said with a nod of satisfaction.

'He is not the man for her. Guy Templeton…'

'Is not the equal of Lovell,' her father finished. 'Lovell is known as the quickest wit in London, just as his father was. Cottsmoor was a genius.'

'The Duke of Cottsmoor.' When they had been alone in the cupboard, Lovell had denied a connection. But how could it be possible to embarrass a man by accusing him of legitimacy?

'His ambitions mesh well with his intelligence. After they have married, I assured him there will be a place for him in government.'

'You had to bribe him to marry Belle?' It was all that Ben Lovell had wanted from the first. How had she allowed herself to forget it?

Her father gave her a surprisingly disarming smile. 'It was not a bribe. It is perfectly natural that I would want to assure my daughter's husband will be successful.'

'And did you assure that Mr Lovell was aware of her difficulties before he agreed to wed her?'

'Belle is a trifle foolish, but no more so than other young girls,' her father argued.

'And I suppose later, when he returns to you and argues he has been tricked, you will tell him to lower his opinion of the female gender to the abysmal level you set for it,' Amy snapped.

'On the contrary, I have nothing but respect for the fair sex,' he argued. 'But there is a reason that you are not allowed to make decisions for yourself, your children or your country. Women are far too emotional to be trusted with the future.'

'So says a member of the gender that has got us into two wars while the factory workers riot in the North,' she said.

'We are not discussing the Luddites,' he said, turning back to the papers on his desk. 'We are discussing Arabella. If Lovell finds some reason to be dissatisfied by the match he has made, then he should have taken the time to know her before accepting my offer.'

'Then you admit you tricked him.'

'I admit nothing of the kind,' he said, reaching for a pen and taking out his knife to sharpen the nib. 'Only a fool thinks all the advantages will be on one side of a bargain. If Mr Lovell was naïve in his expectations about the ease and tranquillity of marriage to Belle or anyone else, then he is no different than all other men his age. Now run along, Amelia. I have business to attend to.'

'And I have needlework,' she said, even more annoyed by the dismissive nod that proved her sarcasm was lost upon him.

Chapter Thirteen

'Lovell!'

Ben quickened his step down Bond Street, in no mood to stop and chat with anyone. His mind was still in an uproar over the turns his life had taken in one short day. He needed peace, quiet and solitude before he could calculate his next step.

Or perhaps he simply needed time to accept the fact that his entire future had been organised by another and done so quickly that he could no longer separate his decisions from Summoner's.

Such a thing had happened to him before, first with Cassandra, then with Cottsmoor. In the end, most things had worked out for the best. He told himself often that the gains outweighed the losses. But he had vowed that, from now on, his life would be his own to plan. And then he'd met Lord Geoffrey Summoner.

'Lovell! Hallo, sir.' Templeton was coming across the street towards him, impossible to avoid.

It took but a second to affix a confident expression that reflected what he should probably be feeling on such a momentous day. 'Hello to you, Templeton. You must be the first to offer me congratulations.'

His friend looked at him with a surprised smile. 'Good news? And I surmise it involves a young lady.'

'You are correct, sir.' He forced an answering smile. He had no reason not to. His fondest dreams were about to be realised. Therefore, he was a happy, happy man. He had but to remind himself of the fact and act accordingly.

'Does the engagement involve a member of the Summoner family?' Templeton responded with playful encouragement.

Ben nodded. 'It hasn't been announced yet, of course.'

'But it is only a matter of time, I'm sure. Special licences are all the rage.'

'I am a conventional man,' Ben countered. A regular licence would take three weeks minimum to read the banns. But if this marriage was what he had wanted, why stall?

'More time to prepare the guest list. It will be the event of the Season, I'm sure.'

'I want nothing less.' Though the prospect of notoriety had appealed to him at the beginning of the Season, now he wanted nothing more than to get the marriage over with as quickly as possible.

Eventually. In a month or so. Maybe two.

'Good for you, my friend.' Templeton was clasping him by the hand, pumping vigorously. 'And congratulations to Miss Amelia.'

'Amelia?' Ben shook his head. 'I am sure she would as soon spit in your hand as shake it. She was none too happy, when she heard the news.'

'But I thought…' The handshaking stopped, as Templeton understood the truth.

'I am engaged to Miss Arabella,' Ben said, fighting back a panicked laugh. It was easy enough to confuse the sisters. He had made that mistake himself while swearing away his future in Summoner's office.

For a moment, Templeton said nothing at all. Was the idea that he'd done as he planned really so shocking? Then the man stuttered, 'B-but you barely know the woman.'

'I spoke to her father,' Ben replied. 'He spoke to me, rather. He summoned me to his house and suggested the match himself.' He still could not decide whether to be flattered or suspicious. 'He had heard of me and wished to further my career. It is only natural that we strengthen the bond with a family alliance. It was exactly as I had planned.'

And yet it did not feel like his plan at all.

'Natural. Yes. I see.' Apparently, Templeton did not see the sense in it either. Though arranged marriages were not the least bit uncommon, he looked as if he had never heard of such a thing, much less seen it happen. 'Lord Summoner called you to his home and gave you his daughter. And now you are seeking congratulations, before you have spoken to the lady.'

'Not as of yet,' Ben hedged. 'I was just down to Phillips to pick up a ring. I will arrange for the licence and talk to Belle directly.'

Templeton withdrew his hand. 'Your cart is not just before the horse. It is miles ahead of it.'

It was true and he knew it. But he could not help but protest. 'Summoner said there would be no problems with the offer.'

'Of course there won't be. When you finally take the time to speak to your fiancée on the matter, you will know why.' Templeton's smile had disappeared. In a few scant moments, he had gone from a picture of *bon ami* to distant reserve.

An unpleasant thought occurred to him. 'Is there some reason that she might be willing to make a match with the first man who asks?'

'You want to know if she is pregnant.' Templeton followed the inappropriate question with an oath before realising that they were on a public street and discussing a lady. His next words were dangerously quiet. 'I do not know whether to laugh, or punch you in the mouth for even considering such a thing. I would call you out, but apparently, it is to be none of my business.'

The last words made no sense at all, but the threat was clear enough. 'I apologise for the assumption. But it was you who led me to it with your vague hints of trouble. If there is nothing to fear, than why have you not answered the question?'

'Because it is beneath dignity,' Templeton replied. 'Arabella Summoner is as sweet and pure as any girl in London. Her only faults are that she is too innocent, too trusting and far too obedient. She will do what her father tells her without thinking of the consequences to her happiness.'

'She will be happy,' Ben insisted. 'I will give her no reason to be else.'

'Because you are supremely confident that you can be all things to all people.' Templeton made no effort to hide the sarcasm in his voice.

'I made no such claim,' Ben argued. 'I only know that my intentions towards the young lady are honest.'

Intentions. Summoner had called him to account for using the word. Why did people find it so unlikely that he could do what he meant to do?

Templeton seemed equally sceptical. His eyes narrowed and his expression changed from aloof to actively antagonistic. 'Very well, then. You mean to do well by her. Perhaps there is nothing I can do to save the girl from all the people who are sure they know what is best for her, but never take the time to ask what she wants. But know that, if I hear you are treating her with anything less than the respect and tenderness she deserves, you shall answer to me. And now, good day.'

But something in his words sounded less like a parting comment than a permanent end to their friendship.

It was afternoon by the time Ben had arranged for a licence. Nearly four o'clock seemed far too late to propose marriage. There was evening, of course. But the Summoners likely had plans and he had anticipated a quiet evening at his club. It seemed a shame to disrupt everything for a formality that could be handled just as easily in the morning.

As he wrote the note of his intentions to call at ten the following day, he could not help imagining Templeton's stern expression on learning of the engagement. Ben had never planned for a love match and nothing had changed his mind on the subject. But the total lack of interest he had in meeting the girl and going through the motions of the offer did not bode well for the future. It was probably Amy's fault. Her continual harping on his unsuitability for her sister must have shaken his confidence.

Or perhaps she was to blame in another way. Last night, his dreams had been of brown eyes flecked with gold. She had claimed that the kiss in Vauxhall was nothing more than curiosity. For her, perhaps it was. From his side, it was nothing less than compulsion. He'd wanted to kiss her. He wanted to do it again. And despite the engagement, he wanted still more.

If his mind had not been clouded by thoughts of Amy as he'd spoken to Summoner, things might have turned out quite differently. He'd have offered for her. And, since it was clear that she did not care for him, she'd have crushed his heart without a second thought as she had all the other men who'd crossed her path. He must not forget the fact. Those few moments in the dark were not heaven. They were a mistake, just as she'd said.

It was with a pleasant smile and a stoic attitude that he arrived at the Summoner home the next morning to take Miss Arabella for a drive in Hyde Park. And, as had been the case every other time he'd tried to meet with her, he came face to face with Amy. Today, she was dressed for a ride, as if she intended to come along with them.

'Miss Summoner,' he said with a slight incline of his head. 'Do not let me stop you, if you are going out.'

She smiled sweetly. 'You are not likely to, since I will be accompanying you and my sister.'

'I do not recall inviting you,' he said.

'Nor would a gentleman assume that Belle could go out without a chaperon,' she countered.

'In this case, it is entirely appropriate,' he said. 'There are things I wish to say to Miss Arabella that are not for another's ears.'

'If another man said it, I might demur,' she whispered back at him. 'But I know from experience how you behave when you are alone with a lady.'

'Was that all some sort of a test, then?' he whispered back. 'If that is the case, then I was not in the presence of a lady at all.'

'You insufferable cad. Are you always so quick to place the blame on another? If so, look no further when wondering why I do not trust you with my sister. Lord knows what will happen when the two of you are together. But I now know exactly what you will say if it is discovered.'

'Amelia!' Lord Summoner was standing in the doorway of his office. The tone of voice he used was harsh enough to quell even his older daughter.

'Father,' she answered meekly.

'You are not making our guest feel welcome.'

'We were just leaving, Father,' she said.

'On the contrary. They are leaving. You are not going anywhere. I wish to see you in my study immediately. Leave Mr Lovell to his business with your sister.'

'But propriety,' she argued.

'Do not worry, Amy. I will take Mellie. He will protect me.' His intended was standing at the top of the stairs. It took but one glance to remember why it was he'd wanted her in the first place. Her golden hair glowed in a beam of morning sunlight, but it was no match for the brilliance of her smile.

Ben gritted his teeth and smiled. 'By all means, let us bring the dog. The fresh air will do him good.' At least it was unlikely to do him harm. Mellie had one of his owner's hair ribbons tied around his scrawny neck, but it did nothing to improve his looks. He ambled down the stairs at Belle's side, tail wagging slowly, watching Ben's pants leg as though he'd just recognised an old friend.

Ben dragged his eyes away from the animal and back to the beautiful woman in front of him. 'Miss Arabella?' He bowed low over her hand.

There was no immediate response to his greeting. Then he heard Amy's hissed whisper. 'Mr Lovell.'

'Mr Lovell,' Belle repeated, like an actor in need of prompting. When he rose from the bow, she made an answering curtsy and gave him a smile that more than compensated for a moment's confusion over his name.

'Might you do me the honour of taking a turn about the park with me in my carriage?' From somewhere behind him, he could feel the eyes of the elder Summoner girl boring into his back. Let her stare. She had tried to prevent both the meeting and the engagement, and failed on both counts.

'I like to take rides,' Belle said, still smiling.

'Then you will like my phaeton,' he replied. 'It is quite high, but you need not worry. I have a very steady hand and the team is well matched.'

'Let us go, then.'

She let him guide her out of the house and to the carriage, as docile as a lamb. She was the very opposite of her sister. When he'd escorted Amy about Vauxhall, he'd had the sense that she'd much rather lead than follow. There was a fierce independence in her, yearning to break free.

This was safer. He smiled at Arabella as he lifted her into the carriage. There was no sense that she was scheming behind that pleasant face, or secretly plotting against him. He would not end the day covered in mud or locked in a closet. Today's outing would be utterly predictable.

There was no logical reason to be disappointed at the prospect of success. Why did he need to keep reminding himself of that fact?

The little dog at his feet was gathering its miserably short legs to jump for the running board and follow its mistress. The attempt was destined for failure, so Ben scooped up the dog and dropped it into the footwell before climbing in after.

The mismatched eyes responded with a look of disapproval that was oddly familiar. He blinked to dismiss it. If he meant to retain his sanity and Lord Summoner's good grace, he must stop thinking of Amelia and measuring one sister against the other. The decision had been made and that was that.

He gave a gentle pull on the reins and manoeuvred them out into traffic, relieved that she was not one of those women who felt the need to talk every moment they were together. Instead, she was unusually silent, staring in wonder at the passing streets as if she had never seen them before. 'It is a lovely day, is it not?' he said to fill the void between them.

She tilted her head towards the sky like a flower leaning towards the sun. A pretty flower. The prettiest flower in London. As he pulled the carriage into the park, he could feel a wave of envy from the people around him and faint whispers of excitement from both men and women. An introduction had finally been made between the two greatest catches of the Season.

The world thought them a handsome couple. As well they should. One had but to look at them to see they were destined for each other.

But the woman at his side seemed unaware of the people around her, still staring up into the sky as though not quite realising that there was nothing left to see. He reached out and touched the tip of her nose. 'If you are not careful of the sun, you will spoil your complexion.'

She giggled. 'That's what Mellie says.'

'Mellie?' He stared down at the dog drooling on his Hessians.

She giggled again. 'You are silly. Dogs don't talk.'

'But…' He looked into the eyes of the dog again. 'Do you mean Amelia?'

Belle smiled. 'Mellie. Amy. My sister.'

'I see.' It was not unusual to have childhood nicknames, he supposed. But he wondered what Amy thought of sharing hers with the benighted beast resting on his shoes. 'And did Amelia tell you why I wished to ride with you?'

'Because you like driving?' she said, giving no clue that she understood.

'Because I like you,' he said, smiling.

She smiled back. 'Then I like you, too.'

He could imagine the caustic response he'd have got from Amy had he begun a proposal with a comment as banal as that. She had likely rejected as many men for insufficient ardour as she had for being too forward.

But he must remember, her sister was different. 'Do you like me well enough to marry me?' he said with a wink.

He waited for her to laugh at his impudence. Even the greenest girl would take such a comment as a joke meant to soften her for a serious discussion.

But this one frowned at him. 'I will have to ask Mellie.'

The last thing he needed was the involvement of the sister who had been trying to sabotage this union since that first night at Almack's. 'On a matter as important as this, I think you need to make up your own mind.'

To this, she said nothing. Then her frown deepened and her breathing quickened as if the act of giving an opinion was pushing her near to panic. After nearly a minute of silence, she closed her eyes and clutched his hand, her grip desperately tight. 'What does Papa want me to do?'

He slowed the vehicle and transferred the reins to one hand so he could use the other to clasp her hand in reassurance. 'I think your father would like you to marry me.'

'Then that must be the right thing to do.' Her eyes flew open. 'But…'

He waited. If she had a doubt in her mind, she had but to say so. She could ask for time to think. She could use any number of delaying tactics and he would happily wait until she was ready. She could even say no if she wanted to.

Then he would be free.

For a moment, he felt just as panicked as she did, waiting for the answer. Then she turned back to him, her face clear but vacant. Her smile was as brilliant as ever, though her eyes still held a hint of worry. 'If Papa wants me to marry you, then that is what I should do.' Then she fell silent again, looking out at the people riding by, as beautiful and distant as a swan in the middle of a lake.

Suddenly, his new fiancée turned to him, smile bright but worried. 'Can I bring Mellie?'

He started. 'Bring Mellie where?' And did she mean the dog or the sister? He was afraid to ask for clarification.

'When we get married and I go to my new house. Everyone says I will have to go to a new house, but no one has told me where it will be. If I bring Mellie, than I shall not be lonely.'

This time he listened, really and truly listened to her words, searching out the meaning of them. She did not say *his* house, nor did she describe it as a home. Listening to her question, his mind imagined a child's drawing of a house, no more detailed than a box with windows and perhaps a chimney or two.

'What else do they tell you about getting married?' he asked cautiously.

'We will go to the church and then have cake for breakfast.' She smiled as if this was quite the nicest thing that she could imagine. 'And then I will go to the new house and have servants and babies and a husband.' Her tone seemed to imply that all things on the list needed no particular order because they were all of equal importance.

Since the beginning of the Season, he and every other man in London had taken her silence as a ploy to attract. But could it be less an attempt to allure than a disguise for something else? Suppose the bright smile on that pretty face existed like an elegant cloth over a plain table, hiding the rickety intellect beneath.

Suddenly, he understood Summoner's demand for an oath and Amy's continual insistence that this marriage would not work. It was not his past that concerned them. It was Miss Arabella. Since she barely understood the engagement, it was unlikely that she would cry off it and give him an easy escape. To break the offer himself would tarnish her reputation and risk revealing to all of London what her family already knew: Arabella Summoner was as simple as a child.

'Well?' She tugged on his sleeve. 'Can I bring Mellie?'

'Of course,' he said absently. 'Bring them both.' Then he turned the phaeton back towards her town house.

* * *

When they arrived at the front door, Belle hopped down to the street before he could come round to help her. Mellie, the dog, was still coiling for the jump, looking down at the cobbles with the dread of one who had too often leapt into situations only to be totally out of his depth.

Today, Ben sympathised. He scooped the dog up again and set him down on the ground so he could scramble into the house after his mistress. Ben followed a step or two behind. He wanted to say his farewell to Arabella and perhaps a few choice words to Lord Summoner on the nature of honesty.

But once he left the house, he would never be able to speak on the subject again. Nor did he expect society to recognise her disability. As long as her looks held, gossip amongst women would be seen as jealousy. And men would likely claim that wits in a woman paled in comparison to the attributes that she already had. There might be rumours that Mrs Lovell was not quite right, but no one would hear them from her husband.

And there, standing just inside the door, was Amy, helping her sister untie her bonnet. Why had he not spotted the real difference between them, from the first? Belle's beauty came from her innocence. Her heart and mind were unaffected by care. It was the simple bloom of an untouched child.

But Amy's beauty glowed from within. It was a complex, difficult, prickly sort of loveliness, more like a wild flower than a rose. But once seen, it could not be unseen. Even as they stood together, his eyes, his mind, his heart, were all drawn to the elder sister and he could not pull them back.

'Belle, darling, do not dally too long in changing out of your walking gown.'

Now Amy was shaking the wrinkles from her sister's coat before handing it to a maid. As she turned, he saw her hair, loose and cascading down her back in a smooth wave. He had thought it an unremarkable brown, when first he'd seen it. But today it shone with the same gold that he saw in her eye. Why did she bother with curls and braids? Did she know that the sight of her undressed hair would render a man speechless with the urge to touch it?

'It is almost time for tea. We are having your favourite.'

Their conversation was mundane, but to Ben it was like music. He had accused her of jealousy and his father proclaimed her a bad influence. But the love Amy felt for her sister wove through the words.

His fiancée turned to her sister, her smile blindingly brilliant as if she heard it as well. 'Jam tarts.'

'Yes, dear.'

'May we have them for supper as well?'

'No, dear. At supper, we need something more sub...stantial.'

He could tell the exact moment she noticed they were not alone by the hitch in her words. She glanced in his direction and favoured him with a smile that was polite, but cool. 'Mr Lovell, will you be joining us?'

Had her father lectured her on her behaviour towards a future brother-in-law? The animosity that had seemed to sizzle between them was gone. And surprisingly, he missed it. What if the passion was gone as well? Suppose there was nothing left but this benign courtesy? 'I can stay but a few moments,' he responded, just as polite. 'But if it would be possible to speak with your father...'

'Unfortunately, he is away from the house. But I can answer any questions you might have. If you care to wait in the salon, I will be there directly.'

He nodded his thanks and made his way to the room he'd waited in on the previous day, before making his devil's bargain with Summoner.

She came to him a few moments later, closing and locking the door behind her. Then, without asking, she went to a cabinet in the far wall and removed a brandy decanter and two glasses. She poured both and handed one glass to him, before taking a sip from her own. 'It is unladylike to admit it, but there are times when a delicate restorative is not enough.'

This was definitely such a time. He drank deeply before speaking. 'You were right.'

She laughed bitterly and took another sip. 'It is a day too late to tell me so.'

'And I swore to your father, on the Bible, no less, that I would not withdraw my offer.'

'There is a reason my father is respected as a

master politician,' she said with a grim smile. 'It would take a smarter man than you to outwit him.'

He knew he should be insulted by her assessment. But since it had been proven true there was no point in arguing. 'What am I to do now?' he said, more to himself than to her.

'I suggest you do exactly as you planned to do from the first. Marry my sister and take the seat in the Commons that is offered you. Perhaps she is not as you assumed she'd be, but she is not beyond hope. She is quite good with some things and hopeless at others, of course. But her temperament is pleasant and she is very, very pretty.'

And she had a sister who knew her strengths and weaknesses better than anyone on the planet. She had learned to display her to best advantage and guard her against peril. It was the reason Belle's entry into society had been such a success. 'You have been keeping her secret, for all this time?'

'For as long as I can remember,' Amy replied. 'In the classroom, I did her work as well as my own so our tutors did not punish her. And it is not really so necessary that a woman be as learned as a man.' She glanced in the direction of her father's office as if she'd got those words from him. 'Men expect very little of us, save that we be lovely.'

'And Arabella is that,' he agreed.

'As are you,' she said, giving him a look that said she had no patience left for handsome but foolish men. 'Marry my sister, retire to the country and raise a mob of perfectly beautiful offspring between you.'

'But, I cannot…' He should have known that a simple life with a quiet woman was an illusion. Nothing with women was ever as it appeared. And in this case, it was not just difficult, it was impossible. Arabella had proven today that it was not a simple matter of obedience that led her to this marriage. She had hesitated when he'd proposed, because she had been searching for the words to refuse him. When she had not found them, she'd been as trapped as he was.

Now they would be wed and she would feel nothing for him other than what she had been told to feel. And when he looked at her, he would feel nothing but obligation.

'There will be nothing wrong with those children, if that is your concern,' Amy said, interrupting his introspection. 'What happened to Belle occurred at the moment of her birth. When she was finally delivered she was blue from lack of air.' Amy tapped her forehead. 'It was not good for her mind. But the rest of her is as perfect as she appears.'

'It is not the children I am concerned with,' he said, horrified. 'Does she even know what is expected of her?' He had never lain with a virgin. He had been told that their first time was painful. No passionate reward could induce him to hurt her. He would never forgive himself.

'Do not worry on that account. I will take it upon myself to explain to her. She will be prepared to do her duty.' Now Amy looked as burdened with obligation as he was.

'And how much do you know of such things?' he said, not sure he wanted the answer.

'There are books on the subject,' she said primly.

'Does your father know you've read them?' He could not decide whether to be shocked or impressed. But for propriety's sake, he was sure he should not be feeling as aroused as he was at the idea of her puzzling over pictures of copulation.

'For the smartest man in London, my father can be woefully obtuse when he chooses to be,' she replied. 'He has no idea what his daughters have got up to, nor does he fully recognise Belle's incapacity. But in the matter of her future, someone had to provide her with the details of her womanly duties.'

'And you took that upon yourself,' he said.

'Among other things.' She shrugged. 'Father means to see her married, whether I think it is a good idea or not.' She paused. 'The plan is not impossible. She could make the right man very happy, and he could make her happy in turn. But the final decision did not rest with me. So, I have been planning accordingly. I did not want to risk her being totally ignorant of the process and terrified by an equally ignorant man who did not care for anything but his own needs.' She gave him a long, searching look, as if trying to decide if he fit that description.

'I can assure you, I am quite capable of putting a woman's pleasure before my own.' He'd had years of experience doing just that, his own needs and desires subsumed by a demanding woman. He'd thought that when he married, he might finally be lord and master. Instead he would be more care-giver than husband.

And worse yet, he was discussing the intimacies of marriage with the woman who he should be treating as a sister. No matter how sophisticated she might pretend to be, her understanding of love making was based on purloined books and a few vague fumblings in Vauxhall. Her cheeks had gone so crimson at his last response that the blush must have extended all the way to her toes.

Which meant that it had spread to all the interesting places in between. He cleared his throat. 'Enough about Belle. What plans did you make for yourself?' But his thoughts of the immediate future had him imagining her skirts around her head as he gave her a practical demonstration of the subject she meant to teach. He shook his head, trying to dislodge the image, and set down the glass, cursing the brandy in his hand for clouding his judgement. 'I mean, what do you mean to do once your sister is settled?'

She cast her eyes down, her face still pink from their previous conversation. 'I decided that it would be best if only one of us married.' She paused. 'It would not be so unusual if Belle took in her spinster sister when she found a husband. Then I would be there to help her with the running of her household.' There was an entreaty hidden in the words, though she tried her best to make them hypothetically innocent.

'No.'

Her eyes flew up to meet his, surprised at the vehemence of his response. 'She is not as feeble minded as you might think, after conversing with her. But neither can she manage alone.'

'I did not claim that she could,' he agreed. 'But that does not mean I want you in my house.' Although he was still not sure that he hadn't agreed to it when talking to Belle in the carriage.

The colour was draining from her face now from the shock of what she must assume was an insult. 'We have had our differences,' she admitted. 'But please, let them end immediately. You are to marry Belle and I will not stand in the way of it. All I want is that she has a kind and gentle husband who will take the time to understand her. You can be that man. I can help with everything else.'

'No.' She was near to trembling with mortification. He wanted to go to her, offer comfort and assure her that it was nothing she had done to make him reject her. But he did not dare, for the same reason he could not have her in his house. 'You are the last person in the world who can help with my marriage to your sister.'

'But why?' She reached out a hand in petition.

He stared at it for a moment, fascinated by the graceful curve of fingers and the way it cut through the space between them. His skin prickled in awareness, as if she was actually touching him. Every nerve came alive to fight against reason for possession of his soul.

Then he looked up, into her eyes. The lashes were spiked with unshed tears. The dark centres were huge, the gold in the left one balanced like treasure at the edge of a bottomless pit. If he claimed it, he would fall. And nothing would ever be the same.

'This,' he said at last and gave in as the pounding tide in his blood battered the last of his resistance to rubble. As he seized her, the empty brandy glass fell from her hand, shattering on a mahogany side table. Then he was kissing her. She tasted sweet and heady like the liquor she'd been drinking. He wanted to drink her in and get drunk on her, as if he was not already intoxicated just by sharing a room with her.

Apparently, she felt the same for she made no effort to fight against him as he loosened the string at the neckline of her gown and let the bodice gape so he could touch her bare breasts. 'Did your books tell you of this?' he asked, tugging her chemise out of the way and taking a tight pink nipple into his mouth, sucking hard.

The answering groan told him what he already knew. Reality was better than any book. Her back arched and he looked up to see the delicate curve of her throat begging to be kissed. He obliged, stroking her breasts with his hands. Then he used them to push her backwards and down on to the divan behind them.

He stopped for a moment to admire the perfection of her, effortlessly wanton and waiting.

Brown hair was wild about her face and her head was cradled on one arm. The muscles of it tugged at one breast so it rode higher than the other, nipple pointed toward the heavens.

If she was painted, just like this, it would result in the sort of masterwork that drove artists mad and made collectors kill to possess it. But he alone would have the flesh behind the canvas. There was no way he could live innocently as a brother to a woman like this.

Perhaps she would learn her lesson, after today. But he feared he never would. It sometimes seemed, the more unattainable a woman was, the sweeter she tasted. To test the theory he went to her, resting one knee on the cushion between her legs, and pushed her skirts to her waist.

'What are you doing?' She tried and failed to make the words sound like a scold, but there was too much eager curiosity in them to warn him away.

'If you don't know, then you've been reading the wrong books.' He ran his hands up the naked thighs above her stockings, then wrapped his arms about them and lifted her to his mouth for the most intimate kiss.

Her body gave one brief jerk of shock before she relaxed and opened herself to his mouth, letting him take her, sweet and salty, musky and wonderful. He eased his fingers into her and took her in easy thrusts as his tongue pushed her to heaven and beyond. And now she was shaking in the throes of orgasm.

Was it her first? he wondered. The first given to her in this way, he was sure. In a few moments, he would be her first in the only way that really mattered. First, last and only. His erection gave an eager twitch at the thought of entering the tight channel that his fingers had found.

Her spasms of pleasure were subsiding. Her eyes were closed tight. Straight white teeth bit her full lower lip. Strands of that glossy brown hair clung to her face. Her gown pooled at her waist, where he'd pushed it, her perfect breasts still tight with desire.

He eased her legs down from where they had been resting on his shoulders, covering her mound with his palm. She opened her eyes again, watching, silent. And once again he balanced on the brink of disaster, unable to pull himself away. 'I do not want you in my house,' he whispered. 'I want you in my bed. I want you in my life. I want you to fill every moment of my future.'

She sighed. The hand that had reached for him before touched his face and he felt it tremble as her knuckles grazed his cheek.

He reached to undo the flap of his trousers.

And then, without warning, the hand that had just caressed him pulled back and struck his cheek, hard, as if to knock sense back into him.

He reeled back, suddenly aware of what he'd been about to do. Then he scanned the room, staring at the windows that faced a busy London street. The curtains were partly drawn, the divan obscured by a corner of the fireplace. Thank God she had locked the door when she had entered. But what if a servant had overheard what was happening? He thought they had been quiet, but it had been minutes since he'd been able to hear anything over the pounding of his own heart and the music of her ragged breathing.

Apparently, she'd come to her senses as well

for she'd pulled away from him to sit up, pushing her skirts down and her bodice up and trying to return to decency. 'You've made your point,' she said, focusing on the arrangement of her clothing, unwilling to meet his eyes. 'I agree. It will be unwise of me to stay in your house, once you have married my sister.'

'If I marry her,' he corrected. Surely after what had just happened, she did not think he would carry through on the farce that they were playing.

'Once you marry her,' Amy said, still not looking up. 'What just happened between us does not change a thing.'

'And why shouldn't it?' At the very least, it had turned his future from difficult to impossible. He could not marry Arabella. Though he had vowed to himself that he would never love anyone again, what he felt for Amy Summoner was not something that could be ignored.

'You made the bargain with my father,' she said, finally looking up and shaking her head in what looked like pity. 'One does not simply walk away from Lord Geoffrey Summoner, after a deal has been struck. You will understand soon enough, I am sure. But for now, you must excuse me, Mr Lovell. I need to attend to my sister's tea. Please, take a moment to compose yourself before you leave.'

Chapter Fourteen

Two years earlier, when Amy had decided that she would never marry, one of the reasons had been to avoid situations just like the one she was in. It had been clear that a future with any of her suitors was likely to end in disappointment.

They all began with the same fine words: compliments, protestations of devotion and promises of future happiness. If she encouraged them, they followed with smouldering gazes, lingering kisses and furtive touches in dark corners. But no matter how ardent they were, their heads turned should another young lady walk past. Only a fool would expect fidelity from them, since many kept mistresses, even as they looked for wives.

If pressed on the subject, they would deny it, of course. They would claim to live and die on her every breath. But when questioned in detail there was no indication that their affection was anything more than physical attraction. They did not seem to *know* her, nor did they show an inclination to learn. The impression they gave was that courtship was a man's game. But once a marriage had taken place, it was the wife's job to learn the husband's likes and dislikes and cater to them accordingly.

If she was to be forced to live her life for another, she'd decided it would be better to live for Belle than for someone who was likely to forget all about her once the thrill of the chase had faded. There was no subterfuge in her sister. Belle loved without condition and without end. If she ever caused pain, she had the sense to regret it and apologise. She was worthy of Amy's devotion.

Ben Lovell was not. He did not even bother to pretend that his ultimate interest lay with the woman he courted. He had kissed Amy one night and offered for Belle a few hours later. Then he had gone back to seducing Amy immediately after he'd got his acceptance.

Even worse, she had wanted him to do it. The

steady heart that she had devoted to caring for her beloved sister was beating quicker at thoughts of the worst man possible. Even knowing that he was engaged to the one person in the world she had vowed to protect, she had allowed him to raise her skirts and prove to her how little she knew about what really went on between men and women. Worst of all, she regretted that she'd sent him away before they had finished what they'd begun.

'Amy!'

She looked up to see her sister holding out her needlework for inspection with the same hopeful smile she wore every day. Perhaps this time her work would be satisfactory. 'Did I do it right?'

'Let us see.' Amy kept her focus on the fabric, unable to look her sister in the eye. 'This bit is all right, but the last will have to be undone.'

'Better, then,' Belle said and put her sewing aside to scratch Mellie's ears.

'Better,' Amy lied and began to rip out the stitches. It was not as if Belle would notice the change, any more than she would notice that Amy was too ashamed to meet her gaze.

I want to lie with your fiancé.

There was no way to make her feelings honourable. Neither was there a way to make Belle understand how horrible it was. Even thinking about what had happened in this very room made her want to melt back into the cushions and touch herself. How was she to explain the details of married life to Belle without thinking of her sister's future husband and imagining herself as the recipient of the skills he had demonstrated on her just a few hours ago?

She returned to her own needlework, staring towards the window instead of at Belle. 'Did you enjoy your ride with Mr Lovell this morning?'

Belle nodded. 'The carriage was very high, but he said not to worry about it.'

'I am sure you were very safe,' Amy said. 'What did you talk about, as you drove?'

'He said he liked me,' Belle said, smoothing Mellie's hair.

'And what did you say to that?'

'I said I liked him, too.' Belle looked up with a confused frown. 'You said before that I should not like Mr Lovell because his pants had holes and he did not like dogs. But I did not see any holes and he let Mellie ride in the carriage with us.'

'I was wrong,' Amy said. 'What I should have said was…' And just what was it she should have said? 'You should be sure that the man you like has your best interests at heart.' It was a good lesson and one that she should learn for herself before lecturing her sister.

'Mr Lovell was nice to me. But I like Mr Templeton better,' Belle said with a definitive nod.

And where was he, now that he was needed? 'Perhaps Mr Templeton was not as nice as he seemed.' If he had lured Belle into the dark walks as she suspected, he had taken advantage of her trusting nature. If he'd meant to do anything more, he should have spoken up when he'd had the chance. Silently, Amy damned the man for his leisurely wooing.

'He was very nice when we were in the Gardens.' Perhaps Father had been right, after all. The secretive smile on her sister's face hinted that it was none too soon to accept an offer, if only to keep her safe from the predatory nature of supposed gentlemen.

'In the end, it does not matter who you like best. Mr Templeton did not offer for you,' Amy snapped. 'Mr Lovell did.' Almost immediately, she regretted her harsh tone. Even if the marriage had been arranged without consulting her, Belle deserved to know that her feelings were important. She asked the next question more gently. 'But I assume he proposed on your ride this morning. What answer did you give him?'

Belle stared down at Mellie, nervously petting his head. 'He said Papa wanted me to marry him. And Papa said I must always obey, because he knows what is best for me.'

And not all syllogisms were true. It was unlikely that she would ever get Belle to understand the finer points of reasoning. It was best not to confuse her with them now. 'So you said yes,' Amy finished for her.

Belle nodded and gave her the same hopeful look she used after crooked stitching. 'Did I do all right?'

Amy nodded. 'I think, this time, you did as well as any of us could have.'

'Good,' Belle said and relaxed a little. Then she

held her dog up, its short legs dangling, and offered him her cheek for a kiss. 'It is all very confusing. But you will help me to understand when I get married and we go to live with Mr Lovell.'

This was even worse than before. 'I know that it was our plan, that I should come to live with you when you married. But now I do not know if that will be possible.'

Belle dropped Mellie on the cushion beside her and stared at her sister in shock. 'But you promised.'

And she had. In all her life, she had never broken a promise to Belle. Why did she have to begin with the one that would most affect her future? 'That was before I realised you would be marrying Mr Lovell.'

'But you said I did the right thing.' Belle's lip trembled with confusion as she tried to reconcile the two ideas.

'You did,' Amy assured her. 'He is a nice man. He will make a good husband.' At least, he would be no worse than the man who had lured her sister towards ruin without honourable intent. 'I just think Mr Lovell will want some time alone with you, after you have married.'

'Why?'

She was nowhere near ready to give the explanation that question deserved. Especially not while she was still blushing from the demonstration of what Ben Lovell did when he got a woman alone. 'I will explain it all to you at another time.' She reached out to pat her sister's hand. 'For now, do not worry your head about the future. You will talk to Mr Lovell many more times before you are married. In no time at all, you will come to like him so well that you will not even need me.'

And perhaps, some day, Amy would not need him, either.

It had been less than twenty-four hours and Ben was back in the same room that had been the location of his emotional undoing. To stand there, even alone, and pretend that he was not thinking of what he had nearly done with Amy was the greatest challenge to composure that he had faced all Season.

In the hours between dusk and dawn, he had

replayed their meeting, over and over, under the pretence of discovering the moment when things had gone wrong. Once he understood it, he could be sure it would not be repeated. Eventually, he'd been forced to admit to himself that the obsession was nothing to do with remorse. It was only an excuse to imagine more and more lurid scenarios where she was willing and he was free to do as he liked with her.

When he tried transferring the fantasy to its correct object, the woman he was going to marry, he could manage nothing more than brotherly affection. She was beautiful, of course. And so quiet and simple that he never need worry about a domineering woman sucking the marrow from his bones, even as he took pleasure in her body. That was what he had wanted, wasn't it?

He'd wanted it before he'd found Amy. Each meeting between them had been a battle of wits. Even when she'd bested him, he'd left eager for the next contest. Her intelligence was as desirable as her body.

Thank God, she was not here to distract him from what he must do. He had seen both Summoner girls turning their horses into Hyde Park as he had driven by it that morning. He'd offered a polite greeting to the pair of them. Amy had ignored him and Belle had smiled and waved, but he saw no evidence that she favoured him over any of the other people she acknowledged, nor remembered that they were to be married in less than a month.

It was just as well. He meant to put a stop to the engagement immediately. The announcement had not yet reached *The Times*. If he cried off now, the whole thing might end with very little embarrassment on either side. Then he had but to explain it to Amy.

She would most likely be angry. She would not want her sister to be jilted, even by a man she wanted for herself. And she did want him. After the incident on the divan, she could not deny there was a mutual attraction. But did she love him?

It did not matter. It would not be the first time he'd developed feelings for a woman who had no heart. Perhaps, this time, passion would be enough. It made no sense at all to fight against something that they could happily succumb to once he had ended his engagement to Belle and offered for Amy instead. It was unorthodox, but it was the only course of action that made sense.

'Lord Summoner will see you now.' The same footman who had led him to the office two days ago was back again to take him on the same short journey down the hall. The great man had the same stack of diversionary papers in front of him to put guests in their place. But Ben had no intention of being put off so easily.

Summoner glanced up with a polite smile. 'Lovell, I did not expect to see you again so soon.' He made a vague gesture to the chair by the desk.

'My lord.' Ben gave him a shallow bow and took the offered seat.

'You have not come to pester me about your future, I trust. The election is not for some time, you know. We can settle the details after the wedding.' His smile, which had seemed wise before, now seemed merely sly.

'It is the wedding that I have come to talk to you about,' Ben replied, his tone and smile free of hesitation or apology.

'You wish a special licence? It can be easily

arranged, you know. I have friends at the Inns of Court. We can have the whole matter settled by evening.' To prove its importance, Lord Summoner put down his papers, as if ready to handle the matter immediately.

Why had he not wondered at the man's haste, when last he'd been here? It had been stupid of him to be flattered by the man's attention and sure of his own merit. The boy he had once been would have known that there was nothing more dangerous to a common man than a smiling and helpful lord.

'I am not here to seek a special licence,' he said. 'I saw no need to rush a matter as important as marriage and do not wish to do so now.' He took a deep breath and said what he had come to say. 'In fact, I wish to call a halt to the engagement.'

The smile on Summoner's face disappeared. 'And I assume I can guess the reason for it.'

'I do not think…'

'You have met my daughter and realise that she is simple minded.'

Ben held his hands up in protest. 'That is not my reason.'

Summoner's eyes narrowed. 'What other reason can there possibly be?'

'The best reason that there is. I do not love her.'

At this, Summoner laughed. 'You are telling me you cannot marry because you do not love? It did not bother you when last we spoke, nor should it have. Do me the credit of finding a better lie than your sudden need for a love match.'

A week ago, Ben would have agreed with the man that love was the last thing to consider when choosing a mate. He had been in love before, or so he'd thought. It had been a disaster from start to finish and an emotion he had hoped he would never feel again.

Then he'd met Amy. And now he was not sure what he felt. He only knew it could not be ignored.

'It is not a lie,' he said, embarrassed by his own earnestness. 'It is the truth. My heart belongs to another. I thought it was still my own when I agreed to offer for Arabella. But…things changed.' It would gain him nothing to explain his confusion on the day he'd sworn, or where he'd been when he had made his decision. 'It would be unfair of me to give myself in marriage if I cannot commit my whole person to the woman I wed. And as a gentleman…'

'If you were truly a gentleman,' Summoner interrupted, 'you would know that marriage in the upper classes rarely has anything to do with love.'

'If I were a gentleman?' If he was a gentleman, he'd have been angry at the slight and not feeling the tangle of emotions that rose at those words.

'We both know who your father is,' Summoner said.

So it was just the matter of his supposed illegitimacy. He opened his mouth to give the usual equivocations that stopped just short of an outright lie.

'We know who he is not, as well,' Summoner finished before he could answer, his smile becoming a sneer. 'I give you credit for being sensible enough not to claim aloud that it is Cottsmoor. You allow people to assume it, but I find no evidence that the story can be traced back to you.'

In the face of such potentially damning evidence, Ben offered a guarded nod.

Summoner continued. 'However, if one bothers to send a man to the village on the Cottsmoor property, one finds Andrew Lovell. From there, it is not all that difficult to discover the truth.'

It was finally over. Though people claimed that hope was necessary to live, the destruction of hope was better than living in dread that it would happen. His future might be in tatters, but Ben felt a tranquillity he had not known in years. 'So you know my past. What do you mean to do with the information?'

Summoner pushed his papers aside to give his full attention to Ben. 'What I do depends on what you do.'

'Knowing what you know, you cannot seriously want me to marry your daughter,' he said. Now that Summoner had the truth, it was unlikely that he could marry either of them.

Summoner smiled again. 'On the contrary. I chose you for Arabella specifically because of what I knew. Men with no secrets are much more difficult to control.'

'Blackmail?' Ben said in surprise.

'Hardly,' Summoner said, with an expression of distaste. 'It is not unusual that I should want to know the particulars of my prospective son-in-law. And as I said before, I had no problems with them when we agreed on the marriage. But I also told you there would be no turning back from an offer, once it was made. You must have known that I had the power to enforce the agreement.'

'I assumed that would not be necessary. My word of honour…'

'Is worthless,' he finished. 'You demonstrate the fact by coming here today.'

'As is yours, sir, if you think you need to use lies and blackmail to catch a husband for Belle. Had I known the whole truth, I never would have agreed to the engagement.'

'Nor should you have considered another, when you were already affianced,' Summoner countered, making no effort to deny his duplicity. 'The previous commitment outweighs the latter.'

'Normally, that would be true. But the heart is not so easily managed as the head. If I cannot treat your daughter with the respect she deserves…'

'You can and you will,' Summoner said in a tone that brooked no further argument. 'You will go ahead with the marriage as planned. What happens after is between you and your wife. If you insist on following your heart?' He gave a cynical shake of his head. 'There is nothing stopping you. If you have not already realised it, Belle will hardly notice should you stray.'

Now it was Ben's turn to be incredulous. 'You are suggesting I be unfaithful?'

'I am suggesting nothing. I am telling you that what happens between a husband and wife is no one else's affair.' His manner gentled. 'All I wish is what I requested from the first. When she leaves this house, she must be secure and happy. You have money enough to keep her safe and she is surprisingly easy to please. Let her keep the damned dog. Buy her dresses. Take her to places where she can dance and eat cake. That is all that matters to her. In exchange, you will have a seat in Parliament and all the advantages I can offer.'

'And if I tear up the licence and end this before it begins?'

Summoner was smiling again. 'Then I will ruin you. Like a Biblical judgement, no stone of your life shall rest on stone. Hurt my daughter and I will make you, your lover and anyone else I can find pay for your perfidy.'

If he took Summoner's advice, he could have them both. But eventually, someone would realise the truth and the scandal would be even worse. Nor could he live with himself if all he had to offer Amy was a clandestine affair with her sister's husband. A woman with such wit and beauty deserved more than just a pitifully secret slice of his life.

It did not really matter if Summoner destroyed him. In fact, the thought was liberating. He would still have the Duke's bequest. It was more than enough to start again. But without Summoner's support, there would still be a scandal. He might be destroying one sister in an attempt to have the other. In the end, he would lose them both and gain nothing.

'Very well, then,' he said, bowing his head and recognising his defeat. 'I will say no more about it. I will abide by my promise to your daughter. She shall want for nothing.'

Summoner's smile returned to the good-natured beam it had been when he entered the room. 'I am glad you have come to your senses. And, of course, I will keep my half of the bargain as well.'

'On the contrary,' Ben said, raising his head to stare, unsmiling, into the eyes of his future father-in-law. 'I will take nothing from you, no matter how willingly it is given. It will not be said that the decisions I've made are based on the bribes of a powerful man. I might lose my heart over this. But I mean to keep my honour as my own.'

With that, he turned and left before Summoner could say another word.

Chapter Fifteen

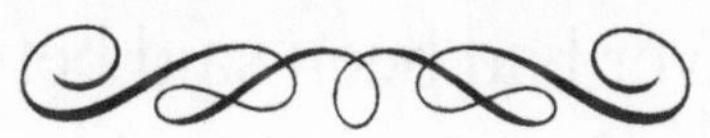

Ben had visited her father. When she and Belle had returned from their morning ride, he had been at the door, collecting his hat and stick from the footman in preparation of leaving. He had greeted them with perfunctory courtesy, a hollow smile and the standard lament that he could not stay longer to have tea with them.

But there was something in the stiffness of his bow that announced he would rather be anywhere than where he was. Though he probably considered himself trapped in a marriage he no longer wanted, there was no sign that he held the bait responsible for his predicament. The smile he gave to Belle in their brief conversation was as near to genuine as he could make it.

In Amy's opinion, it spoke well of him. No matter what he thought about his future, he would take good care of her sister. But his feelings for her father were clear enough, if one bothered to look. Before he'd left, he'd cast a brief look of undisguised loathing down the hall towards the office. Whatever had been said between them, it had not gone as Ben Lovell had hoped.

Amy was not surprised by the fact. She had warned him on the day before that if the deal had been done, there would be no escape from it. Like all men, everywhere, he had not been willing to take the word of a mere woman on something that would have been painfully obvious had he known Lord Geoffrey Summoner as well as she did.

Now he understood. He hated her father. And though he did not love her, he harboured no ill will towards Belle. But for Amy he seemed to have no feelings at all. He had hardly looked at her, though they'd been standing scant feet apart. Words and his smiles had been tossed in her direction as if he wanted her to think nothing had changed between them. But when she'd tried to catch his eye, he had looked past her, through her, or at anything else but her.

Perhaps yesterday's torrid interlude had meant nothing to him. Maybe he was embarrassed that it had happened at all. But if she'd been expecting some acknowledgement that it had been more than a moment's diversion, she was to be disappointed. It was over and they would never speak of it again.

It proved that she had been right all along about men. They thought no further than their own needs, unless forced to do otherwise, as Ben had been by her father. It was all the more annoying that a part of her would always wonder if Ben's response to her today might have been different had she had allowed him to finish what they'd started.

It was a sign of weak character that she was thinking about that at all. If she had any regrets, they should be that she had not put a stop to things much sooner than she had. What had happened was unchaste, undignified, unladylike…

And wonderful. She sighed.

At the sound Mellie, who had been dozing on the hearth rug of the parlour, looked up and growled at no one in particular.

'Silly dog,' said Belle, tossing the last bit of her biscuit to him and setting her tea cup aside.

'Do not spoil him,' Amy said, stretching out her foot so she could rub his exposed belly with the toe of her slipper.

'I still have not taken him to the park to play ball with Guy,' Belle said, staring out the window as if hoping that the gentleman would appear.

Amy frowned. And there was another fine example of manhood. They must consider themselves fortunate that they had stopped him before he had irretrievably compromised her sister. Though he had been all but underfoot for the entire Season, they had seen no trace of Guy Templeton since the incident at Vauxhall, four days ago. Hopefully, the formal announcement of the engagement would be enough to scare him away permanently.

But none of that made it any easier to explain his absence to Belle. 'Now that you are to marry Mr Lovell, you will not be able to socialise with other men as you used to.'

'We are not going to socialise,' Belle said, looking at her as if Amy was the one who did not understand. 'We will be playing with Mellie. And it is not other men. It is just with Guy.'

And there was another problem to be corrected. 'Now that you are engaged, you must go back to calling him Mr Templeton.'

'But he said I should call him Guy,' Belle said, clearly confused.

'Things have changed between you since then,' Amy said, as gently as possible. 'Mr Lovell would not like you being so informal with another man.'

'But Mr Lovell is Mr Templeton's friend,' she offered hopefully, sure that this would make a difference.

'No one's friendship is that strong,' Amy replied.

'When I see Mr Lovell, I will ask him if it is all right.' Belle was clearly not convinced.

Just then, a footman entered with the afternoon post. At the top of the stack was a letter from Mr Benjamin Lovell. It was addressed to The Misses Summoner. Amy stared at it for a moment, afraid to break the seal.

If the contents were in any way personal, he would not have addressed it to both of them. But that did not keep her from wishing that it was a *billet doux.* When she had been actively courting, no man would have had the nerve to send such a thing to Lord Summoner's daughter. But if she was to spend her life alone, without even Belle for company, it might be nice to have a stack of ribbon-bound letters to remind herself of what might have been.

It would be even better if they were written in Ben Lovell's elegantly masculine hand. She stared down at the folded paper in front of her, memorising each line and loop of the address, focusing on the sight of her surname. Without thinking, she ran a fingertip across the words, imagining the forceful pressure of his pen to the paper.

In response, she felt a rush of heat, sudden as a lightning strike. It coursed through her body to settle in the wet place between her legs. If this was all it took to make her want him, than he had been right. There was no way they could reside under the same roof. Even if nothing happened between them, ever again, people would have but to look at her to know what she wanted from him.

Now he'd sent a letter. It was better that it go

directly to his intended, if only to teach Belle that future communications between them did not have to be shared. Amy took one last look at it, then handed it to her sister. 'Mr Lovell has written you. Open it and see what he has to say.'

Belle cracked the wax that held the paper closed and looked at it only a moment before handing it back with a confused shrug. 'Help me, Amy.'

No wonder she needed help. The tidy script on the outside degenerated into a confusion of crossed writing inside. Why had he bothered to turn the paper on its side to write the second half of the missive? There was no need for economy. They could more than afford the postage for a second sheet of paper.

She looked across at her baffled sister. Belle sometimes had trouble deciphering a regular letter, if the writer did not have a clear hand. Separating one direction of writing from another was far too difficult for her to manage. To send such a letter, Ben might as well have been writing in Latin.

Or in code.

There could be no more innocent way to get a private message to her than this.

'What does it say?' Belle was eagerly awaiting her half of the letter.

'Let us see.' Amy smiled at her sister as if the paper in her hand was just ordinary social correspondence and not the most important message she had ever received. Then she looked down, forcing herself to focus only on the first part of the letter, making no effort to let her eyes dart to the left to read the sideways writing crawling in and out between the words. 'It seems we are invited to a house party at Mr Lovell's estate in Surrey.'

'A house party,' Belle said, her worry over Guy Templeton forgotten. 'I have never been to one of those.'

'No, you have not,' Amy agreed, glanced down at the letter again and then tucked it into her pocket so as not to be distracted by it.

'What will it be like?'

Extremely difficult for all concerned, thought Amy. But she continued to smile. 'This one is to celebrate your engagement to Mr Lovell. I suspect there will be fine dinners, parlour games and perhaps a ball where you can meet his friends.'

Belle would be under the scrutiny of everyone there for several days. Since she was the guest of honour, they could hardly creep away home if things got too difficult. Amy grew tense just thinking about it.

'Dancing and games,' Belle said happily.

'It will also be a chance to see your new home,' Amy said with as much enthusiasm as she could muster.

'And I will get to see Guy again,' she said. Then she remembered she was not to be familiar and added, 'Mr Templeton.'

'Perhaps,' Amy said, hoping that, after Vauxhall, Ben would know better than to trust him.

'And it will be your new home, too,' Belle finished, smiling as though relieved that it was all settled.

Amy wet her lips. 'After you are married, things might be quite different than you expected. Still good,' she added hurriedly. 'But different.'

'I like things the way they are,' Belle said, with a surprising show of independence.

'I know, dear. But we cannot always have things the way we want them.'

Belle frowned, trying to understand.

'For one thing, even if Mr Templeton is there, you must not go off alone with him, as you did at Vauxhall. You must not go off into the dark with any gentlemen. It is not a polite thing to do.'

'It was bad to go off with Guy?'

That answered the question of what had happened when she had disappeared. Belle had been alone in the Dark Walks with a man. And despite what she'd hoped of him, Guy Templeton had not stepped forward to make an offer or done anything else to prove that his intentions toward her had been serious. 'You did nothing wrong. It was my fault for encouraging you to spend so much time with him.' She had been so sure that a proposal was imminent that she had thought there would be no harm done.

'It was all Mr Templeton's fault,' Amy said, firmly, knowing it was her own fault as well. 'And I am sure Mr Lovell would agree with me.' He would not like it any more than she liked to think of Ben kissing Belle. 'But you must not let it happen again.'

Belle gave her a doubtful look. 'When we see Guy at the house party, I will ask him if we did wrong.'

Amy looked back in surprise. It sounded almost as if her sister had disagreed with her. If that was true, it was the first time in ages she had heard anything like rebellion. 'You should not even speak to Mr Templeton,' she said, in a firm tone. 'And in no case should you listen, if he tells you to do something. From now on, you must let Mr Lovell make these decisions for you.'

'But what if I do not want to do as he says?' It was a legitimate question and one Amy had asked herself many times, when forced to follow one of the many rules that men expected women to abide by. Men were not always right. And when they were wrong, it was stupid to follow them.

But it was a very different matter when Belle was the one who wanted freedom. 'Mr Lovell is to be your husband. It will be his duty to decide what is best for you in all things.'

'Papa makes decisions for me,' Belle said slowly. 'And so do you.'

Amy nodded.

'And now Mr Lovell will.'

Amy smiled, relieved that she was beginning to understand.

'When do I get to decide things?' Belle asked.

It was a question Amy had hoped that she'd never hear, for she did not have a good answer to it. 'We all want what's best for you,' she began cautiously. 'And on some things…the very important things like marriage…what is best is that you let the people who love you make the decisions.'

'Then why does Mr Lovell get to do it?' Belle's smile had disappeared. Her lower lip jutted out in a pout that would have been unattractive on any other face. 'He likes me. But that is not the same as love.'

For someone thought to be simple, her sister had an excellent grasp of the current situation. 'He is a good man,' Amy said, still not sure if that was true. 'He will take good care of you.'

'But he does not love me,' Belle insisted. The lip that had pouted now gave a warning tremble.

'Love is not really all that important.' Even as she said it, she knew she did not believe it. Love was the most important thing there was. If it was not, then why did it hurt so much when one did not have it?

Belle recognised the lie as well. And for the first time in ages, she dissolved into tears. 'Liar.' She pointed a finger at Amy. 'Guy says love is all that matters.'

'And where is your precious Guy, now that you need him?' Amy snapped, tired of hearing his name. 'If love was so important to him, he would have been the one to offer for you. But he did not. It was a mistake to let him anywhere near you.'

'It was not!' Belle wiped the tears from her face with the back of her sleeve. 'Mr Lovell is the mistake. And so are you.' She gave a loud sniff, trying to clear her running nose. 'He does not love me. And I do not love him. You cannot make me marry him.' With that, she was out of her chair and running towards her room.

'Belle!' It took only an instant for Amy to drop her needlework to follow. But Belle had outdistanced her easily, taking the stairs two at a time.

By the time Amy had gained the landing, she heard the slam of the bedroom door.

'Belle!' She knocked and then pounded, trying the door to find that it was locked. She gave it a futile rattle, as though wanting would be enough to make it open. She had the key in her own room. It would take only a moment or two to run down the hall and get it.

But that had never been necessary before. The door had never been locked. Nor had it been slammed. Even when it was closed, she was seldom on the wrong side of it. She had kept the room key safe and untouched, just as she'd kept Belle safe for eighteen years. And now everything was falling apart.

She knocked on the door again, harder this time. 'Do not be a child, Belle. Let me in.'

But Belle was not being childish at all. She was acting like an adult. She had been all but sold to a man she'd never met. And when she'd had the audacity to question the decision, the person who loved her most in the whole world had lied to her and dismissed her feelings as unimportant.

'I am sorry that I did not listen to you,' Amy said, running her fingers over the panel of the locked door. 'Come out and we will talk.' Then she could explain again, but better, this time. And then everything could go back to the way it had been and they would be happy.

But that was not true, either. No amount of explaining could take them back to a time before Ben Lovell. Nor could it make Guy Templeton into the sort of man who was worthy of her sister.

'I know this is hard to understand,' she began again. It was hard to explain as well. 'But this marriage is for the best. You cannot simply lock yourself in your room to avoid it.' Nor could they drag her down the aisle and force her to marry a man she did not want. All the plans she'd made for the pair of them had been based on a willing and agreeable Belle. She had sacrificed her own life to that end, knowing that, even if she had no one else, Belle would always love and need her. What was she to do, if Belle no longer wanted her help?

She stroked the door again, as if it were possible to transmit the comfort through the wood to the person who needed it. 'Have a good cry. Later, when you are feeling better, come to my room and we will talk.'

Then she walked slowly down the hall to her

own room, near to tears herself. What was she to say or do that would make any of this better? It had always been her job to take care of Belle. She was always there to make sure things did not go wrong and to fix them if they did. But how could she fix something that was just the way it had to be?

Perhaps Ben Lovell had an answer. It was his ambition that had brought them to this point. He should take some responsibility for the misery he was causing. He had been so kind, when they had been together in Vauxhall. If only he were here to help her.

Then she remembered the letter in her pocket. As Belle had done, she locked her door, wanting to savour the moment of reading, whether it brought pleasure or pain. She unfolded the paper again and turned it on its side to read the second half.

Amy, dearest,

I have no right to call you such. And yet I cannot help myself. No matter what you feel in return, to me you are and always will be dearest.

I have been trying to find the words to ex-

plain my behaviour towards you. But there is no justification for what I have done and what I would do in the future if the opportunity presents itself. I cannot see you without wanting you.

Please accept my apology for the liberties I took. I know how you responded to another who overstepped himself. And I have earned far more from you than the blackened eye you gave to Haines.

She stopped to smile and touched the letter to her lips before reading more.

I am promised to another and bound by oath to the current course of action. The engagement is unbreakable as you warned me it would be. But when I am with you, I forget all that. Honour has no value. The future has no meaning. I only see the moment. I only see you.

Though you might not want me, if I could find a way to free myself, I would run to you. Perhaps you would cast me off as you did the other men who courted you. Even if it cannot be, you will always have my heart.

But the rest of me is promised to another. Please, for the sake of your sister, accept the invitation to my home. As I made clear on our last meeting, sharing a household would be disastrous. But we must find some way to be sure that your sister has the help she needs in her new life.

It will not be easy for either of us, but we must both do what is best for Arabella. I swear, I will not trouble you, as I have in the past. It will be best if we try, as we should have from the first, to abide by the constraints of society and make use of a chaperon, for the sake of your reputation and my peace of mind.

She smiled again. Once, he had said he did not need peace. Now that it was gone, he had changed his mind. One could almost feel sorry for him.

I eagerly await your answer to my invitation and your attendance at my home.
With love,
Ben

She held the letter for a moment, unwilling to admit that she had reached the end. It was everything she could have hoped for. He burned for her, as she did for him. He had called her his dearest and offered his heart.

He had offered his love in the closing, but that was hardly an uncommon way to end a letter. There was no point in either of them saying that particular word too often. With things as they were, it could mean nothing but pain. It was far better that the feeling they shared was something far less permanent, a flame that would burn itself out once they stopped feeding it.

But for now all he needed from her was an answer to his invitation.

She read it through again. Then one more time so she would not forget the words. And then she went to the fireplace, searching for one remaining ember from the previous night's fire. She dropped the paper upon it, watching the edges blacken and curl. From any other man, it would have been the perfect keepsake of a brief, romantic interlude. But such words from her sister's future husband should not exist in anything more concrete than memory. In a moment, there would be nothing left to prove they had ever existed.

When the paper had all but disappeared, she seized the poker and dragged the last scrap away from the flames, picking it up and patting the glowing edges until her fingers singed. The bit that remained had an L, an O and part of a V. The E that would have finished the word was little more than a shadow of ash.

She went immediately to her jewel case and found a locket to hide it in. Once she had closed it up, she gave it a brief kiss before clasping the chain around her neck.

Only then did she sit down at her writing table to write a response to Mr Lovell's brilliant suggestion of a house party. The words were polite, prosaic and completely unsatisfying.

Chapter Sixteen

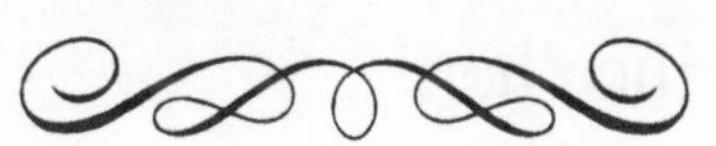

The journey to Ben Lovell's country house was largely uneventful. With Parliament in session, their father politely declined the trip, citing too much work in town to take even a few days away.

After her brief excitement at the thought of a party, Belle continued to brood about the impending marriage and her lack of control over her own future. It took almost a full day after their argument before she was willing to leave her room and even longer before she spoke to Amy. She complained of pains in her stomach and insisted that Miss Watson bring her meals upstairs, and replied in monosyllables, even if Amy avoided the subject of marriage.

When Amy reminded her of their need to pack for the house party, so they might set off on the morrow, Belle flatly refused. Though the thought had excited her as they'd read the invitation, she now declared she was far too sick to leave the house. When all of her usual tricks to manage Belle had failed, she was forced to appeal to their father to convince her.

He had called Belle to the office and closed the door before Amy could follow her in. There followed almost an hour of ominous silence. Then the door had opened and Belle had emerged, white faced and teary, but prepared to go to Surrey the next morning.

Amy breathed a sigh of relief at this partial return to normal. But while there was no more talk of stomach aches and wanting independence, there were fewer smiles as well. Belle was still answering most questions put to her with a shrug and announced that it did not matter what she wore and that they should simply pick the first dress in the cupboard and be done.

The final straw had been when Miss Watson had declared herself a victim of Belle's imaginary illness and taken to her bed, unable to accompany them. This left Amy to organise both of them, their maids and enough luggage for a week's worth of parties in Belle's new home. She could have left it to the servants. But the more she thought about the letter she had thrown into the fire and the man who had written it, the more anxious she became.

While Belle had decided to do nothing, Amy found it was much easier to occupy herself matching hair ribbons to gowns and deciding if it might be necessary to take the large trunk and not the small one. Then they would have room for their habits, in case there was an opportunity to ride.

She would make sure everything was perfect, just as she always did. Then, perhaps, Belle would be happy again. The time was fast approaching when she would have to abandon Belle to her new life. And what would become of either of them, after that?

For now, she imagined a dozen ways to keep herself busy that did not involve talking with the master of the house. She hoped that Belle's new home had grounds to explore. Perhaps there would be a chance to visit the nearby Royal

Botanic Gardens. She could leave one of the maids to watch over her sister and escape for a while.

There might be a library that held books she had not yet read. If there was a music room and sheet music, she might attempt to teach herself a new tune on the pianoforte. Her skills were little better than adequate, but that was probably reason to seek improvement. Beyond that, there were cards, games, needlework…

But suppose the house was small and ill suited to entertain? Suppose, wherever she went, she saw Ben? It would be hard enough being in his home and learning the intimate details of it. If she was near him, there would be a constant threat of intimacy. She never should have agreed to the trip.

But then she reminded herself of the perfectly reasonable request in the letter. They were doing this for Belle's sake. She must learn to love her new husband and the man she was to marry. No amount of talking had put an end to her rebellion. But if this brief and painful trip was needed to convince her, then Amy would make the best of it. There was nothing she could not attempt, if it meant that Belle would be happy again.

* * *

The roads were dry and they had made fair time, pulling up the sweeping drive to the house less than an hour and a half after leaving the Summoner town house. She had not meant to be impressed by his home. But if Amy's only concern had been to place her sister in the nicest house, it would have been impossible to deny Ben Lovell her hand.

The structure was new and had been designed by no less than the great John Nash, himself. The majestic symmetry of the white limestone walls was framed by terraced gardens and carefully trimmed boxwood hedges.

The well-ordered building was tended by an equally efficient staff. Footmen and butler greeted them with warmth and were spiriting their luggage above stairs before they had even come down from the carriage.

The tall front door opened on to a breathtaking hall with spotless marble floors and ivory walls rising to a vaulted ceiling trimmed with gilded rosettes and wreaths.

But while Amy viewed it with wide-eyed admiration, Belle reached out for Amy's hand, clutching it in fear. 'Mr Lovell lives here?'

Amy patted her hand to comfort her. 'Yes, dear. And soon, you will live here too. Is it not beautiful?'

Belle shook her head. 'I do not like it. It is too big. Too big and too white.'

'That is not such a bad thing,' Amy whispered. 'But if you tell Mr Lovell it does not please you, he will let you repaint it, I am sure.'

'It will still be white underneath,' Belle said, not moving.

Amy took her hand, tugging her forward over the threshold. 'It is bigger than our house, to be sure. But that does not mean that it is not a nice place. And I doubt you will live here all year.'

'There will be more?' Now Belle looked truly helpless, unable to comprehend how her small, secure world had become so large and strange.

'He has rooms in the city and will likely get a town house once you are married. And if he means to stand for Parliament, perhaps he will have a house near our land in Dorset.'

While Amy felt a perfectly reasonable envy at

the idea of three fine homes, Belle could manage to do nothing but shake her head in denial.

'Welcome, ladies. Please come in.' Ben was coming down the stairs towards them, his midnight-blue coat a perfect foil for the austere design of his home. As his eyes met hers, the flame of envy in Amy's heart turned into a raging covetous fire. It did not matter that he was to marry Belle. He was hers and always would be. Without thinking, she stroked the chain of the locket and the scrap of love that it contained.

When he took the last steps down to their level and came towards them, his eyes were focused upon her sister. At her hesitant smile, he got the same stunned expression that all men wore when confronted with Belle's full attention.

Then he bowed low and took her hand, kissing the knuckles. 'Welcome, Arabella. Please, treat my home as your own, for thus it will be.'

For the first time in days, Belle's foul mood improved and she smiled back.

'Let me show you about the house, while your rooms are being prepared. Then, after you have refreshed yourselves, I will introduce you to my friends. They are all eager to meet you.'

Ben offered his arm to Belle and after a brief hesitation she took it and let him lead her out of the hall. Amy followed a pace or two behind, regretting each step. It had been a mistake to accompany Belle here. She should have forced Miss Watson out of bed and sent her instead. She might have stayed in London for the Season's festivities.

Perhaps it would have looked odd when she did not attend her sister's engagement ball. But society was used to thinking her odd. It did no harm to her reputation to reinforce that opinion with her actions.

Anything would be better than spending the next few days feigning approval as Ben escorted Belle about the grounds, rode with her, danced with her and fostered the intimacy necessary to make a happy union. Even the affection she felt for her sister was not without bounds. It was one thing to sacrifice the man she loved and quite another to pretend to be happy as she did it.

Ben escorted the Summoner sisters on a tour of what was to be the home of one of them. The wrong one, of course. It was too much to hope that it might be home to the pair of them, just as Amy had always planned.

He had told her it was impossible. He knew in his heart that it would be. But he could not help hoping that she would ignore him and come anyway. If she did, he would not be able to send her away.

Maybe this week they could find the restraint that had been lacking in their previous encounters. If they could aspire to a platonic relationship, he would be spared the terrible emptiness he'd felt as he'd written the letter. Even if he could not have her, he could still see her. It was something, at least.

At the moment, Belle was on his arm, following with less spirit than Mellie the dog. If she was impressed by the size and modernity of his home, he saw no sign of it. If anything, she looked frightened.

One step behind them, Amy kept up a running commentary on his tour, pointing out the smoothness with which the kitchen ran with no help from the master, the spacious bedrooms and the pleasant view of the gardens where Mellie could chase rabbits while his owner sat in the shade of the oaks.

Did she actually like the place, or was she only encouraging her sister? Damn his pride, but it was important that she be impressed. But she sounded no more attached to it than an agent hired to rent the house.

'If you like dancing,' he reminded Belle, 'you will find the ballroom delightful.' He opened a door and brought them out on to the little balcony that had been designed to hold the musicians. The sound of their voices echoed through the room below.

'Think of the lovely parties you will have here, Belle,' her sister said coaxingly. 'And you will dance every set.'

It was likely not true. As hostess, she would have to attend to the happiness of her guests before her own. But the idea that she might dance here brought back the sparkle that had disappeared from her smile. 'We will dance here tonight,' he agreed, 'After the rest of the guests have arrived.'

'I would like that,' Belle agreed hesitantly.

Now that he knew her better, her beauty did not have the same, devastating effect on him that it had. Was it really so easy to become jaded with perfection? Or was it simply that she was not the one who had been meant for him?

When had he begun to crave a love match? He had learned when he was much younger that love was a dangerous business. Life was better when one was not caught and suffering like a fly in a web, about to be devoured by the teeth of one's own passion.

He had come to London well aware that love was not necessary for a successful marriage. He wanted tranquillity. And he might still have it, if he learned to take satisfaction in the smiles of the pretty but simple girl.

There were likely many tricks to making her at ease. He would need Amy to teach them to him for it might take years to learn them on his own. If he could have her here, just to talk to…to explain…

And there he was again, standing on the edge of a cliff and wanting to jump just to feel the wind in his hair as he fell. If he could not even turn around to look her in the eye without being near to overcome by lust, his future was not likely to be full of innocent conversations about her sister's happiness.

'Ben?' The young voice came from the doorway, directly under the balcony they were standing on. Belle stepped forward to peer cautiously over the edge, wondering at the source.

'In the gallery, above you,' he called, then turned to the girls, leading them to the steps down to the main floor. 'I have been looking forward to this moment for some time. I would like to introduce you to a special friend of mine.'

It was hardly fair to the boy who stood at the foot of the steps, watching their approach. Even travel-weary, the Summoner girls were intimidatingly beautiful. Despite his recently acquired *sangfroid*, John was still, underneath it all, a fourteen-year-old boy, struggling with the same feelings that showed no more mercy to kings than they did to bootblacks.

'Your Grace.' Ben bowed. 'May I introduce my

fiancée, Arabella Summoner, and her sister, Amelia? Ladies, his Grace the Duke of Cottsmoor.'

For a moment, he was caught between mutual expressions of owl-eyed wonder on the faces of John and Amy. Belle seemed to understand that she should be in awe. But from her expression, she could not get past the fact that the person who should demand her respect was also barely out of leading strings.

Amy regained control after only a second or two and executed a perfect curtsy. 'Your Grace.'

A single glance to her side demonstrated to Belle what was expected of her and Belle duplicated her sister's greeting.

John was the slowest to regain his wits. He looked from one to the other, then managed a clumsy bow, 'Miss Summoner,' he said, turning to Belle. 'Miss Arabella.' The second bow had a hitch in it, as though someone had punched him in the stomach to make him bend.

But it was far better than he'd have managed at that age. Ben smiled at the boy, unable to disguise his pride at the success. Then he rescued them all from awkward silence. 'Cottsmoor has agreed to take a few days from his studies to celebrate with us.'

'We are honoured, Your Grace,' Amy said, with a smile almost as charming as her sister's.

'It is I who am honoured,' John said, looking from one to the other. Then he looked back to Ben in an incredulous aside. 'This is your fiancée?'

'Try not to sound so surprised,' he said, smiling. 'But indeed, I have been very fortunate.'

'We just met,' announced Belle. 'But now we are engaged.'

Inserting the unvarnished truth into a polite conversation was always a hazardous thing. This one brought the exchange to a dead halt.

It took only a moment for Amy to recover, and give the John another one of her brightest smiles. 'We consider ourselves fortunate as well, Your Grace. Mr Lovell is quite well known and well thought of. He does credit to your—'

He could tell by the panicked look in her eye that she had been about to say family before she remembered that the common rumour that they were brothers was both rude and untrue. It took less than an eye blink, for her to finish with '—patronage.'

John had not noticed the hesitation. He had been too busy staring at the gold light in her eye that so fascinated Ben. Proof that the boy had excellent taste in women. Then he pulled himself free of her influence long enough to answer, 'I have known Ben my whole life. I consider myself just as fortunate to have his counsel.'

They were headed towards the usual awkward pause, as Amy realised that she could think of no conversational topic worthy of a peer. It was a shame. Though John longed for ordinary human interaction, he had already learned that a few moments of Cottsmoor was all the average person could stand.

For a moment, he shifted from foot to foot, displaying a child's eagerness to hold the attention of adults. Then he steadied himself and the Duke reappeared. 'We must talk further, this evening,' he said, with a surprisingly adult smile. 'I look forward to dancing with you both, since, clearly, you will be the loveliest ladies present. And now, if you will excuse me?'

'Of course, Your Grace,' Ben said. And, after a brief exchange of bows and curtsies, he was gone.

If and when she ever got Benjamin Lovell alone, Amy would give him her opinion on surprise visits from the peerage. It had not been the most mortifying conversation of her life, but it had been one of the most difficult.

When the boy was properly out of earshot, she turned and pulled her sister aside for a whispered scolding. 'Belle, in the future, you must not speak so candidly about the circumstances of your engagement, especially not in the presence of Mr Lovell's friends.' By the innocent expression on her sister's face, there had been no malice intended. But that did not make it right.

'It was the truth,' Belle said, quite reasonably. 'Miss Watson says we should tell the truth and shame the devil.'

'In this case, telling the truth shames Mr Lovell.' Of course, when they were alone together, he was the devil. It made Belle's logic irrefutable.

'You did not shame me,' he said softly from behind them, making Amy cringe in embarrassment.

'You were not supposed to hear that,' she said. She'd assumed there was enough distance between them for her comments to pass unnoticed.

He gave her an innocent smile. 'As I said before, the acoustics in the ballroom are excellent.' Then he looked to Belle. 'Do not concern yourself. Cottsmoor found you both quite charming.'

'He was a nice boy,' Belle agreed.

'But in the future, you must remember that he is a very important man,' Amy reminded her.

'And, since he is male, he is just as susceptible to your charms as the rest of us,' Ben said, with a tone of finality. 'Do not trouble yourself, Amy. If you smile at him, he will forgive you anything.'

If Belle knew nothing else, it was how to smile on command. To end the conversation she did exactly that. Ben smiled back at her and held out his arm. 'Let us continue our tour.'

Now that she had seen most of it, it was apparent that her initial assessment had been accurate. The house was perfect. Annoyingly so. Just like its owner. It was also impossible for Belle to manage without help, just as its owner would be.

It was a shame that looks were not enough, for

they made the most handsome couple imaginable, walking arm in arm, in front of her. And Ben was doing his best to be the man who was required. He was solicitous of her sister, trying to interest her in the many advantages to the place and tempting her with jam tarts and dancing. He even pointed out a window seat in the library that would be a perfect spot for Mellie to nap.

But if he meant to have a seat in Parliament, he could not also be at home helping his wife to navigate the complexities of married life. Mere good intentions would not be enough. But it was unfair to suggest that he stay away from his own house and allow her to resume her place as Belle's right hand.

And though she was pleasant for the Duke, no matter what Ben did to please her Belle moped from room to room to room, not saying a word. It was not until they passed through the front hall again that her mood improved.

'Guy!' At the sound of his voice in the entryway, Belle pulled free of her fiancé's hand and galloped down the hall toward the open door.

'Miss Summoner.' Guy Templeton turned at the sight of her, bowing deeply.

She ignored the formal greeting and took both of his hands in hers. 'It has been forever since I've seen you.'

'Only a few days,' he replied, laughing.

Amy came into the room at a slower pace, not wanting to show the alarm she felt at the sight of Belle's enthusiastic greeting. 'Mr Templeton,' she said, catching his eye to give him a warning glare. 'What are you doing here?'

The smile he returned was as innocuous as ever. 'I was invited. I have a house not a mile from here and I am a good friend of our host. It is hardly a surprise.' He gestured toward Ben, who was still standing in the doorway.

'You are a good friend of my sister, as well,' she said, watching carefully for his reaction.

'That I am,' he agreed.

'And this is still my house,' Ben said quietly beside her. 'I will invite who I choose to visit me. And Templeton is not just a good friend. He is my best friend.' He stepped forward then and offered Mr Templeton his hand, which forced him to release Belle to accept it. 'So good to see you. We will have far too many unpartnered ladies tonight. I cannot be expected to dance with all of them.'

'Guy is a good dancer,' Belle announced. Apparently, the recent lecture on discretion had gone unheeded.

'You flatter me, my dear.' Templeton smiled at her and held her gaze for longer than was necessary.

'I am sure Mr Lovell is a good dancer as well,' Amy said, trying to get her sister's attention.

But Belle did not turn away from Mr Templeton. 'I do not know. I have never danced with him before.'

In a lifetime of caring for her sister, Amy had learned to think of her disposition as placid, docile and agreeable. But never before had she been so consistently contrary for such a long period of time. She looked helplessly at Ben, readying another apology.

He warned her off with a slight shake of his head and then said, 'That is true, Belle. But we will dance tonight and you will be able to judge for yourself.'

Then he turned to his friend. 'It is clear that my fiancée is eager to speak with you, after so much time apart.' He continued to smile as if there was nothing untoward in Belle's reaction. If there was irony in the statement, it was very well concealed. 'Perhaps you can be the one to escort her about my gardens. You know them almost as well as you do your own.'

'I would be honoured.' Templeton responded with a bow that was a trifle too formal to be given to a close friend. 'Miss Arabella?' He held out his arm to her.

Her sister embarrassed herself yet again by responding with such a relieved sigh that he might well have been rescuing her from a dungeon and not her own future home.

When they were gone, she turned to confront their host. 'Are you sure that was wise?'

'Allowing my best friend to escort my fiancée on a tour of the grounds?'

'Some might say you are too good a friend in return,' Amy said. 'He was your rival before the engagement.'

'As was every other man in London,' Ben responded.

'But none of the other men were such particular favourites of my sister,' she reminded him.

'Perhaps so. But I have faith that he will honour her commitment to me,' Ben said.

It was surprising that a man who seemed so worldly could be so naïve. Amy rolled her eyes. 'You trust him. Very well. But now that she is engaged, Belle should not be cultivating the attentions of other men.'

'You make your sister sound quite calculating, Amy. We both know that she is not.'

'It is not a matter of subtlety,' she said. 'It is quite the opposite. She barely understands the effect she has on men, much less knows how to use it. It is why I have been guarding her so closely.'

'And now it will be up to me to protect her,' he said with a sigh.

Which meant that her job was ending. What would Belle do without her help? And what was left for her, if there was no Belle to give meaning to her life? She could imagine nothing ahead but emptiness. 'I do not think she is ready to be married,' she said. 'Many things have changed for her in the last week.'

'For all of us,' Ben agreed.

As far as Amy could tell, the biggest change was that they were all less happy than they had been. 'I have been trying to explain things to her,' she said. 'I must make her understand that you will be good to her and that what is happening is for the best. But until she is used to the idea of your marriage, it is best not to give her false hope.'

'Is marrying me really such a repellent prospect?' For a moment, he sounded genuinely hurt.

'You know it is not that,' she said softly.

He nodded and turned toward the stairs. 'Let me show you to your rooms. Then you may go and retrieve your sister from the dangerous Mr Templeton.'

He was treating the situation as a joke. She opened her mouth to tell him so and to make him understand the risks involved with leaving Belle alone, even for a moment, with a man who could no longer be trusted.

And then she reminded herself that it was no longer her business. Belle did not want her help, nor did Ben. They would have each other, for better or worse, just as the ceremony said. And she would become the spinster everyone thought she already was. With time, her opinions would hold even less value than they did now. In time, they might forget her altogether.

She took a deep breath to banish the self-pity and followed Ben up the stairs to the bedrooms. Her room he called the blue room. It was charmingly decorated and looked out over the garden. She glanced down to see her sister and Mr Templeton in animated discussion next to a plot of rosemary.

'See? They are perfectly safe together.' Ben was standing behind her, looking out as well. He was close enough that his breath stirred her hair as he spoke.

They were together, alone. And her bed was only inches away. She stepped away from the window and went quickly toward the door. 'They are safe together, but we are not.'

He followed her out into the hall, shutting the door behind them. 'I am sorry, Miss Summoner, I meant no offence.'

Of course, he had not. Neither had she. And yet they had been about to forget themselves, just as they did each time they were together. She nodded an acceptance of the apology. 'Show me Belle's room so I might go to the garden and fetch her.'

Before something terrible happens.

At this point, she was no longer sure whose virtue most needed guarding. But it might be best if she stayed at Belle's side for the rest of the visit.

Ben was standing before the next door and removed a key to unlock it. It opened on a room far larger than the blue room beside it, decorated in a cream and gold scheme very like the entryway below. By the size of the large canopied bed and the connecting door on the far wall, it appeared that Belle had been given the room reserved for the lady of the house.

Ben saw her raised eyebrow at the nearness to his bedroom. 'I thought it best that she be given the same room she will inhabit when she comes here after the wedding. I do not want it to seem strange when we…' He faltered as if unwilling to think the next words much less speak them aloud.

When you share a bed.

She did not want to think about it either. The time was growing near when she would have to explain it all to Belle. And just the thought of that conversation made tears trickle down the back of her throat.

Without another word, Ben removed another key from a ring in his pocket and handed both to her. 'In case you are concerned about the connection to the master suite, here is the only key to it.'

She responded with a solemn nod. 'Thank you, for your thoughtfulness.' She slipped the keys into her pocket. As she felt the weight of them dragging at her skirts, she could not help wondering if either of them opened the door to his room as well.

Chapter Seventeen

The evening was as perfect as he'd promised it would be. Despite the fact that there was no lady of the house to see to the menu and the decorations, the ballroom was charmingly arranged and the supper delicious. He had hired musicians from London who performed in all of the best households.

The guest list included half a dozen couples along with John, Templeton and the Summoners. It was almost too intimate to be called a ball. But for Belle's first visit to his home, it would be better to start small.

He had done well.

And beside him, staring at the room in wonder, was his reward. Arabella Summoner wore a gown the colour of a maiden's blush. The sheer muslin was bound by gold cords that crossed between her breasts. A matching gold cord wound through her fair hair. She was a goddess come to earth, so beautiful it hurt to look at her.

Her sister was a much more cerebral deity, an Athena to her sister's Aphrodite. She'd dressed in warm brown silk, a colour that hardly seemed festive enough for such an occasion. But when she turned to look at him, he saw that it matched her eyes. The gold of the locket at her throat echoed the light shining in them. Tonight, there were no plumes or braids to spoil the long, tawny hair and no fan to hide her lovely face. He could stare into that face for ever.

He did not dare to. He dragged his eyes away from her and turned to smile at Belle. 'Is it to your liking?' He waited, breath held, for her answer.

After what seemed like weeks of trying and failing to catch Arabella Summoner, now that he had her, he approached her warily. It was as if she was an untamed cat and he expected to be scratched. It was nonsense. There was not a tamer creature in the room than the woman he was about to marry.

But cats sometimes scratched because of fear. That was what he sensed from her now. At his words, her beautiful head dipped and, though her eyes darted nervously about the room, her smile was as bright as ever. But it was ruined now that he knew how little there was behind the artifice.

'The ball,' he prompted. 'Do you like it?'

'Yes, thank you,' she said, automatically.

'We will be expected to dance the first waltz,' he said, offering her his arm.

Her head tipped to the side.

'You have not waltzed?' Of course she hadn't. She was young and it was still too improper for the likes of Almack's. He gave her an encouraging smile. 'I will teach you. It is a very simple dance.'

'I like to dance,' she said. He had begun to think it was as much a ruse to hide a lack of conversation as a statement of truth. But at least she was not as blunt as she had been that afternoon. Perhaps she was growing accustomed to him.

'So your sister says.'

Belle gave him another worried look. 'She says I must obey you in all things.'

'That is the way marriages usually work,' he

said, surprised that he would have to explain it. 'If Amy marries, she will obey her husband, just as you should.'

'She will not like that,' Belle said. 'Amy likes to give orders, but she does not take them well.'

He could not help himself. He laughed. 'You are wiser than they give you credit for, Arabella.'

'Thank you,' she said automatically.

'And you must try not to worry too much about our future together.' He would do all the worrying for both of them, just as Amy had done. 'For now, all I require of you is a dance.' He took her hand to lead her to the centre of the room. 'Here. Let me show you how to waltz.' He lifted her hand in his and put his other hand on her waist.

She stared down at it as if trying to decide whether this was an actual dance, or a trick to make her behave improperly.

'Now you put your hand on my shoulder.'

Her touch was tentative as she rested it there, but at least they were positioned correctly.

'Watch my feet. Step, step, step. Step, two, three. Do as I do. But with the other foot. My right, your left.'

They managed a few tentative steps in harmony with each other and he gave her another smile. 'Very good.'

She smiled back at him with a relieved sigh, then tried to detach her hand from his.

He shook his head. 'Now we will dance around the floor in a circle.' He nodded to the musicians, and they struck up the first notes of the Sussex Waltz. When she did not immediately follow his lead, he set them off with a rocking first step that would have been more appropriate in a polonaise than a waltz.

She succumbed to the momentum of it, only to falter again as he made the first part of a turn. Though he had thought it instinctive, apparently the process was more confusing than he'd assumed. Or perhaps he was not a very good teacher. She was pressing back against his hand instead of yielding to its direction and they faltered on another step before finding the rhythm again.

They managed quite well for a few measures and he was beginning to hope that the worst was over. But then, other couples came to the dance floor to join them. Her head tipped again, a posture he was beginning to recognise as confusion, rather than flirtation.

It should not have surprised him that the new pattern was baffling to her. When one was accustomed to dancing in matched lines and staying with the set, a jumble of bodies making lopsided circles within circles must seem like nonsense.

She was fighting against his lead again, trying to see what was happening around her rather than letting him do the watching. The ribs beneath his hand felt as immovable as corset bones, though he was sure under her delicate gown there could be but the most cursory of stays.

It was all the more annoying to see Templeton pass them in a graceful spiral with Amy in his arms. They danced so naturally they might have been created as partners like Meissen figurines come to life. The sight should not have annoyed him. They were nothing more than close friends enjoying the hospitality of his home. Their smiles were a sign of his success. And success was what mattered after all. It was why he was going to marry a woman he did not love who did not want to follow his simplest instructions.

You must be patient with her.

It was Amy's voice in his head, reminding him that this was to be his life, from now on: one part husband, one part father, one part teacher. He had no right to be frustrated if Belle could not keep up. He would need to slow down and help her.

Templeton was about to pass them again. Instead, he paused with a smile. 'Might we change partners, Lovell? It seems forever since I've spoken to Miss Arabella, and I have not had the opportunity to congratulate her on the nuptials.'

'You spoke with her just this afternoon,' Amy said, eyes narrowed. 'You had ample opportunity for felicitations then. Besides, I do not think changing partners in the middle of a dance is allowed.'

Which was better: a woman who had trouble following instructions or one who refused to do so? He had told Amy not to fuss over Templeton and Belle, but she could not seem to let it alone.

It was either that, or she preferred to partner with Guy instead of him. Were both of the Summoner girls so afraid of him that they could not dance him? It was one thing to keep a safe distance and quite another for Amy to be appalled at the idea of his touch. He smiled stubbornly at her. 'As host and hostess, the rules are what we wish them to be. And I say we should switch partners.'

Apparently, his fiancée wanted to obey him, after all. By the time he looked to Belle for her opinion, she was already stepping clear of his embrace and holding out her arms to Templeton. In a show of propriety, he held her more loosely than Ben had done. Perhaps that had been all that was necessary. The pair of them set out together as gracefully as Guy had danced with Amy.

Ben stared after them for a moment, annoyed. Then he heard the sound of a clearing throat about the level of his first waistcoat button.

When he looked back, Amy was staring at him expectantly. 'Are we going to dance? Or are you going to wait until they come round again so you might trade back and be rid of me?'

'I apologise.' He scooped up her hand and they set off, spinning easily about the room. 'I was just noticing that Templeton is a better dancer than I am.'

'As someone who has danced with you both, I beg to differ,' she said. 'But if it improves your mood to have me abuse you on the subject, I will be happy to accommodate you.'

'That will not be necessary,' he assured her, irritated that she might be right about Templeton and Belle.

It was some comfort to find he had no trouble at all dancing with Amy. She responded effortlessly to his guidance, matching him step for step. 'You are an excellent dancer,' he said, trying to focus on the steps and not the nearness of her.

'A better dancer than my sister?' she said in a dry tone.

'She was unfamiliar with the waltz,' he replied.

'She does well enough with your friend,' Amy goaded. 'In the future, perhaps you will take my advice and be less eager to push her into his arms.'

'Don't be so dramatic,' he said, glancing across the floor to see Belle laughing in the arms of his best friend. 'One last dance is hardly a reason for concern.'

'Are you sure it will be the last?' she said. 'You are neighbours, after all. She will see him again.'

Of course she would. Templeton dined here once a week, at least. If Ben stood for office, with or without Summoner's help, he would not have the time to guard his wife.

'You are beginning to see the problem,' Amy said, nodding in satisfaction. 'You heard her today. She views you as a stranger. As such, she feels no real loyalty to you. But after Vauxhall, we both have reason to distrust Mr Templeton.'

'I am sure they are guilty of nothing more serious than a few kisses,' he said.

'Some might say the same of us,' she reminded him.

It took nothing more than the mention of what they had done to send a rush of blood through his body, stirring the desire that had lain dormant. The woman he wanted was already in his arms. It would take nothing more than a tightening of arms to pin her body against his.

And Summoner's horrible suggestion whispered at the back of his mind. He could keep them both. One for his mind, his heart and his body, and the other for the illusion of perfection that his future demanded.

Belle would not expect fidelity. Neither should he. What did it matter whose arms his wife slept in, while he was lying with another? If they could not all be happy, there was no reason that they might not at least be physically satisfied.

It might not have been the marriage Miss Arabella imagined for herself. But that was because she was a naïve child and her sister was not much better. But it would not take so very much to kill their innocence and bring them both to their senses, so the four of them could live comfortably.

Most importantly, a man could not let his life be ruled by romantic nonsense, if one intended to do great things. Humans, both the male and the female, were nothing more than animals. They had an animal's desire to rut and breed. Only when that biology was appeased could the mind be free for higher thoughts.

He stopped, dead in the middle of the dance floor, disgusted by his own thoughts. But they were not *his* thoughts at all. *He* knew that humans were imbued with divine virtues: reason, honour and temperance. They were what separated a man from a beast.

Ben knew that. But old Cottsmoor hadn't. He had spent half his life trying to escape the worst of that man's teachings. Tonight they had all come back at once, ready to claim his soul.

'Mr Lovell?' Amy was staring up at him in confusion, waiting for him to move. When he did not she whispered more urgently, 'Ben?'

'Excuse me.' He dropped her hand and released her, walking from the room without another word.

Chapter Eighteen

Amy stared at the canopy over her bed, trying to forget the evening she had just endured. The days leading up to the trip had been difficult enough, what with Belle's sudden change of disposition. Relocating her and presenting her with this *fait accompli* of a marriage complete with house, servants and friends in the peerage had only made it more complicated.

When Amy added the feelings she held for the host, her troubles multiplied exponentially. But really, it had been going quite well, all things considered. Other than that brief moment of temptation while looking out the bedroom window, she'd been the picture of decorum. For a moment, while they'd been dancing, she had actually convinced herself that something like a normal friendship might be possible.

They had been talking. It had been their usual, squabbling banter. Then, with no explanation, Benjamin Lovell had gone mad. There was no other way to explain it. He had stopped dancing. Instead of laughing away the pause, he'd stood stock still for almost a minute and grown so distant that she feared she might be witnessing the beginning of an apoplexy.

With even less warning, he had come back to himself, offered the briefest apology and abandoned her on the dance floor. His behaviour had been so bizarre that it took a moment for her to notice her own humiliation.

She was standing alone in the centre of a crowded room, staring after him. It did not take long before the other dances stopped as well. And then the music stopped and the whispering began.

Lovell had been dancing, not with his fiancée, but with her sister. The first dance was not even finished. What had he said? What had she said? What could possibly have happened to bring about such a bizarre turn of events?

When Mr Templeton noticed what had occurred, he went to search out his friend and demand that he attend to his guests. He returned a short time later to whisper that Mr Lovell had shut himself up in the library with the brandy bottle and would not be returning.

Showing surprising presence of mind for one so young, Cottsmoor announced that the host's indisposition was no reason that the rest of them could not still enjoy themselves. He demanded that the musicians begin again and partnered Belle at the head of the set for Brown's Reel.

Her sister was delighted. She was also the only one who did not seem at all concerned by her fiancé's absence. But her renewed vivacity was enough to keep the male guests on the dance floor and the evening was salvaged.

Tomorrow, perhaps Amy could find Ben and scold him for acting the fool. He'd got exactly what he'd wanted, after all. Though it gave her no real pleasure to be proven right, she had told him from the first that it would never work. If he had refused to listen, he had no right to complain.

Belle would learn to adjust. Despite her nonsensical worries about the whiteness of the walls, she could be happy here. It was a beautiful house, modern and well attended. The servants seemed nice, as well. Perhaps they would recognise the deficiencies in their new lady and fill the gaps themselves. In a place like this, Belle could find a way to manage without her.

The thought brought another swirl of emotions. After a lifetime together, she was about to be parted from the sister she loved. She should not be feeling relief that someone else would be taking over the burden of care. Belle could not help how she was. And what good did it do Amy to be set free when no one was left who wanted her?

She should be happy that Belle was to be married and not jealous. This was no different than those childish tears she'd shed when her baby sister had got a toy that she desired, even though it was clear that Belle lacked the ability to appreciate it. It had been unworthy.

But, no. This was worse. They were both full grown and the man she wanted for herself had been handed over to her sister. Amy was left to help them start a life together, before stepping demurely out of the way. There was a limit beyond which sisterly devotion could not pass. She had always imagined that it would be death. That their final parting should be because of a man was something she had never suspected.

In the darkness, she heard the hall door open and close again. She did not know whether to pray it was him, or pray it wasn't. She held her breath until his silhouette hovered over the bed.

'What are you doing here?' she whispered, even though they both knew.

'I came to apologise,' he said.

'Then you may do it in the morning,' she said primly, pulling the covers up to her neck. 'When you do not reek of spirits.'

'In the morning, I will not have the nerve to say what needs to be said.'

'Your cowardice is not my concern,' she said.

'So says the woman who used to hide behind her fan each time I spoke to her,' he said and sat down on the edge of her bed.

'What good would a few ivory sticks do me, if my closed bedroom door did not stop you?'

'It was not locked,' he said.

To this, she had no glib riposte. She had not locked it because, in her heart, she had hoped he would come to her, just as he had. 'Then state your business and leave,' she said.

'First, I must tell you that, on the day your father sent for me—'

'And what day was that, precisely?' she said, in no mood to hear about men and their plans.

'The day after Vauxhall,' he said, with a trace of impatience. 'I—'

'He sent for you?' She sat up in bed, trying to see his face in the dim light.

'He invited me to your house,' Ben said. 'I assumed he had heard what we had been up to, the night before. I was prepared to offer. But—'

'Offer? For me?' All this time, she'd assumed he had come to carry out his original plan without a thought to the kiss they'd shared.

'If you insist on interrupting, I will never be able to finish,' he reminded her.

'Very well, then.' She gestured to cede him the conversation, then bit her lip to keep from interrupting again.

'I came to your father, ready to make amends.

And when he began talking of a betrothal, I assumed…' Now he was the one to pause. 'We were talking at cross-purposes. He kept insisting that you had no interest in marriage, especially not one he might sanction. And before I knew it, I was engaged to Belle.'

No matter what his original plans had been, he had not been the instigator of the sudden and bloodless engagement. Why had she not recognised her father's hand in it, from the first?

'And now you must think me an idiot,' he said with a sigh. 'But you must believe me when I say, it was you. It has always been you. I did not want it to be. But it has been you from the first moment I looked into your eyes at Almack's.'

And even though she knew she should send him away, she held out her arms and he came into them, burying his face against the side of her neck to kiss her pulse. 'I had plans,' he said, with a shaky laugh. 'But they are a handful of dust, compared to how I feel, when you are in my arms.'

'How clever of you to notice now that it is too late.' She wanted to be as sharp and cutting as she had been in their first meetings. But what was the point? There was no fight left. She had lost. She ran her fingers through his dark hair, urging him on, even as she knew she should push him away.

'It is not too late,' he argued. 'Tonight, as we danced, I realised that I cannot go through with a loveless marriage to your sister. It is not fair to her, any more than it is to us.'

To us.

Only two words, and yet they were even more seductive than his kisses. She must ignore them.

'And what will become of her, if you cry off? The scandal will be on her head more than yours.'

'She will not be hurt,' he whispered as his fingers twined in her hair. 'I promised your father that and I promise you the same.'

'How will you accomplish it? And even if you can, what am I to do about Belle? Someone must care for her, no matter what happens. She is my baby sister and she needs my help.' Should they decide to marry, if that was what he intended for her, taking Belle into their house would be just as awkward as if Amy had tried to live with them. Even if he cried off, there was no way that they could all be free to start again.

Finally, after so many years of being strong, she broke. She had not cried in ages. But suddenly tears were spilling down her cheeks faster than she could wipe them away. She took a breath to gain control of herself and it emerged in a sob.

He needed to go. If he would just leave her alone, perhaps she could still pretend that there was nothing between them. And tomorrow, when the brandy wore off, he would rethink his words and the wedding would go on as planned, with her standing at her sister's side as witness.

But he must not do what he was doing now.

He had climbed into her bed and was holding her racked body to his, kissing her hair and running his hands over her shoulders, trying to soothe the sobs that were coming faster and faster as she finally allowed herself to cry. 'Let it out, my love. It's all right.' He pressed his lips into her jawline and she felt her muscles working against them as she tried to swallow the tears.

'It's not all right.' And she was not his love. She could not be without hurting Belle. She shook her head to dislodge his kiss. 'It has never been all right. Father refused to believe there was anything wrong. I tried to make it seem so, for his sake. For both their sakes. But it has been so difficult. And now?' She gave a helpless flap of her hand. 'This.'

'You are not alone anymore.'

She felt a strange shift deep inside as if, with a few words, he had managed to lift the heavy load that had been weighing on her soul.

'I promised to take care of her,' he said. 'And I will do so to the best of my abilities, no matter what happens.'

Her tears were slowing now and she raised the sheet to dry her eyes. She felt him reach into the pocket of his dressing gown to get the handkerchief he was pressing into her hand. Then he shrugged out of the garment and lay naked beside her.

No matter what happens.

The words sounded ominous. If there was a new plan forming, she suspected she would not like it. But she did not want to think about the future as he rolled to cover her body with his. 'This is wrong.' She made a last, half-hearted effort to push him away, but he held her fast.

'It is not prudent. But it is not wrong,' he said. 'In fact, it is the only right thing in the world.'

'You are only telling me what I want to hear,' she said. And doing what she wanted him to do. Beneath the hem of her nightgown, his bare legs tangled with hers. Warm arms were wrapped around her body and she could feel every muscle. Her cheek rested against the smooth skin of his shoulder. The feel of so much flesh pressed to flesh made her dizzy with desire.

'Do you want to hear that I love you?' he said. 'Because I do. And I never wished to love anyone, ever again, because it hurts.'

He was right. It did. Though her body rejoiced, her still heart ached.

'Please,' he said softly. 'Let me know you, even if it is only for one night.' The words sounded like goodbye. And if they were, this could be their last chance to be together.

Without another thought, she turned her face to his and kissed him, open mouthed and hungry, letting passion burn the pain away. When they broke, minutes later, they were both panting, eager to be as one.

'I was lost from the first moment I saw you,' he said, reaching down her body and stripping away her nightgown to leave her as naked as he was. 'Those incredible eyes. One look and I was yours. I will never be free of them.'

That was good. She did not want him to be free. She wanted him to be hers. Though they were in darkness, she saw into his heart and was not afraid. His hands were stroking her breasts and she could not keep from moaning at the pressure of his fingers. The eager sound came from an untouched place, deep within her.

He reached between their legs, rubbing her until she was wet for him. His hands on her were rough and hurried, but she did not mind. She ached with wanting him. The punishment of being without him could only be relieved by an equally punishing joining.

She raked her fingers down his sides, scraping her nails down his flanks until she could reach no lower. Then she brought them back up again to the crease at the back of his legs, clutching the tight muscles of his buttocks as they tightened for the first thrust.

And then he was inside her and she would never be alone again. He was hard as stone, stretching her body to the point of pain, but it did not matter. As he pounded into her, she sank her teeth into his shoulder to muffle the cries of desire. She wanted to mark him, to claim him as he was claiming her so that no other woman could have him without knowing that he belonged to someone else.

Perhaps it had been too much. He withdrew suddenly, leaving her empty and longing. Then he grabbed her again, rolling her, arranging her body as if she was a puppet and he her master. He pushed her up on to hands and knees, then grabbed her waist to steady her and took her from behind, like an animal.

He hunched over her and one hand wrapped around to stroke her in time with the short, sharp pumps of his hips. A final touch and she surrendered to him, totally and completely, her overwhelmed senses making her shudder with relief as he surrendered in return.

She collapsed forward on to the bed and he followed her down, on top of her, inside of her, part of her. Then slowly, they rolled to the side, skin to skin, his arms wrapped around her and a leg slung over her hip. Thus, they drifted towards exhausted slumber, nestled together, tight as spoons in a silver drawer.

Chapter Nineteen

Ben lay in bed watching for a change in the darkness of the room. Soon, it would go from pitch black to coal. Then the beginnings of grey would creep in at the edges of the curtains. Before that happened, he would need to be gone. He could not be seen leaving her room when the first servants woke to begin their duties.

It was as good a day as any to destroy a man's reputation. But the woman involved…the women, he corrected…must remain as near to untouched by scandal as he could manage.

Amy was beginning to stir as well. They had made love once more during the night, slowly, quietly, each knowing that this might be the last time. When they slept again it was side by side. The distance between their bodies was slight, no more than an inch. But to Ben it already felt oceans wide.

He could feel her beside him, pretending that she was still asleep. But her tiny hand rested against his chest with too much weight to do it unconsciously. She was trying to bind him to her not with strength, but with the weight of her longing.

It was an interesting feeling. Women had held him in bed with tears, both of sadness and rage. He'd been seduced, threatened, begged and, on one particularly memorable occasion, restrained by ropes. But he had never felt such hesitant need. It was like a flower trying to hold on to the sun. To know that such a fragile creature depended on him for happiness made him feel strong, invincible to an almost godlike degree.

He wished it could never end.

Her head rested in the hollow of his arm. He could see her eyes were open now. There was a glitter of wetness on the lashes, as the first hint of daylight touched them. She reached up to stroke his cheek. 'You love me, do you not?'

He could see the lines of her face now, so classically pure in form that he could barely stand to look at them. She was beautiful. Not the equal of Belle, but her superior. Why had he not noticed before, when there had been more time?

It was the eyes, he suspected. He'd been so caught up in their appearance that he'd never looked past them to the woman within. While Belle might have a sweet soul, it was childlike and untouched. But Amy had seen things and known them and been marked by them. She was ageing, like wine, and he longed to drown himself in her.

'If you do not love me,' she whispered, 'then lie to save my feelings. I will not feel so foolish, then. I will tell myself it could not be helped because we were in love.'

Light or dark, perfect or ugly, she had not changed from the first day he met her. He laughed. 'You are not supposed to suggest such things. It is unfeminine.'

'To request that you lie, or to pretend to believe you when you do?' she asked.

'Either, I think,' he said. 'And I am finished with lying, for all the good the truth is likely to do me. I love you, Amelia Summoner.'

'Says a man who has no heart.' She sighed.

'It must have grown back, but it is beating as if it might break.' He covered her hand with his and moved it so she could feel the thumping in his chest. 'I love you,' he said again, enjoying the sound of the words.

'And I love you,' she said, nestling closer to him. 'Why does this not make everything easy?'

'If we were the last people on Earth, it would.' He laid a hand on her bare hip, wishing that there were more time so that he might love her again before they had to part.

'Go to my father and tell him you cannot marry Belle. You must—' She stopped suddenly, as if realising that she could not be the one to demand a proposal, she could only agree to it.

He thought of the destruction it would bring to his reputation and to Belle's should he cry off. The idea fascinated him. To be able to stand in the ruins of his old life and start again. 'If I left her, would you be there, waiting for me?'

'I could not love a man who hurt her,' she said without hesitation.

'So, your answer is no.' He felt another part of

him break. 'You do not have to worry. There will be nothing left of me to marry. If I break the engagement, your father swears he'll ruin me.'

The sweet woman in his arms let loose with a most unladylike curse.

He laughed, in spite of himself. 'He wanted to protect your sister. He was afraid, once I knew about her, I would abandon her.' The oath to Summoner was a growing weight in his gut, crushing the air from his body and ruining the moment. But, at least, now he understood the need for it.

Swear that you will never hurt my daughter.

Amy could fend for herself, but Belle needed protection.

'If either of you had listened to me in the first place...'

'You were right, all along,' he agreed.

'It would be better to be happy than right,' she said.

It was true, but it did no good to think about it. 'I swore,' he repeated. 'And it would be better if my word had any value. But it does not. No matter what I swore, I cannot follow through on it.'

'If you jilt her, she will be ruined as well.' Amy's voice was bleak as she realised the truth.

'It would be even worse should I cast her off to marry you,' he agreed. 'But there is a way out.'

For some of us, at least.

'Let us take it, whatever it is,' she said hurriedly.

'First, I must tell you a story.' And he had best do it quickly. The room was getting lighter by the minute. 'Once upon a time, there was a foolish young man…'

'Do I know him?' she asked playfully.

She still had hope that the ending was a happy one. He swallowed the shame that welled in his throat and went on. 'He was the son of a cabinet maker. His father died leaving him without money or prospects and a widowed mother to care for.'

She made no answer in response. It made him wonder if a horror of such an ordinary birth had stunned her to silence.

'Then, one day, a beautiful and powerful woman caught sight of this young man…who was little more than a boy, really…' Seventeen had been old enough for some things. Wisdom was not one of them. 'And they entered into an arrangement.'

'Who was the lady?' It was barely a whisper.

'You will know the truth soon enough.' He tightened his hold on her hip, waiting to see if she shrank from his touch.

She did not pull away.

'And you and she…'

'I came to help with the apple harvest,' he said, 'hoping to be paid in windfalls.' His mind wandered back to the distant autumn day he'd first seen Cassandra. 'She was taking an afternoon ride, when she saw me.' And he had seen her, golden in the slanting sunlight. The memory of it still made his body quicken after fifteen years.

'You must have been very handsome,' Amy murmured, as if she could picture the scene herself.

'And she was very beautiful. I loved her,' he said. It had been true, at first. 'I could not help it. She was magnificent. Charming and witty and not too many years older than I. And there were advantages to the arrangement.' Other than one that his loins had noticed from the first.

'You were not educated abroad,' she said, her voice flat.

He laughed in surprise. 'If that is what you take from my confession, you are very innocent indeed. No, I was not formally educated, in this country or another. But it is amazing what can be accomplished when one wishes to impress a woman and has access to a library.' He could still remember those early days, alone with all those books and the feeling, almost like hunger, for all the things he did not know.

'I read,' he said, simply. 'And I questioned. And then I read some more. But there are still so many questions left unanswered. Why are some men dukes, and others common? Why do some men make the laws when others can only be punished by them? The system is not ordered by their innate wisdom or lack of it. I have seen that it takes little more than a decent tailor and a set of proper manners to pass amongst the upper classes unnoticed.'

'But people think you are Cottsmoor's son,' she said, obviously still stunned.

For a moment, he wondered if she meant to cry out the truth and see him cast down into the depths that had been his future, to work with his hands and keep his eyes and mouth tightly shut so that he might not upset a divinely ordained system. 'It began as a joke between the Duke and his wife,' he said. 'He said I was there so much, I might as well be family. To spite him, she told someone I was his son. To spite her in return, he agreed and encouraged me in my studies.'

'He knew about you and…'

'…his wife,' Ben finished for her. 'He did not care. They loathed each other. Cottsmoor and I became quite good friends. But the better he liked me, the more she hated us both. And yet, she did not want to let me go.' And then it had been too late for him to get away. 'My love for her died, long before she did.' He had stared down into the grave and felt nothing but relief.

'By then the world was convinced that you were a duke's son. You acted like one, at least.'

He shrugged the shoulder that supported her head. 'I am sorry to disappoint. But it is better to be thought a bastard than known as a paid satyr to a lady of importance.'

'And the resemblance between you and the Duke?'

'Purely coincidental,' he replied. 'But my family has lived on the Cottsmoor lands for generations.

It is possible that a previous duke hid a natural son close by and there is some distant blood connection.'

'And he encouraged you to exploit it,' she said and then fell into silence.

'If he'd thought I could carry it so far, he'd have been just as likely to see me swing at Tyburn. But he is not here and I am.'

'And planning to stand for office,' she finished.

'After a long acquaintance with a member of the House of Lords, is it so surprising that I might want to use the education I gained to see that men like him are not the only ones making the laws?'

To this, she had no response. If this had been enough to shock her, he did not dare tell her the rest of the truth. But he did not want her to be disgusted with him. He wanted to hear her reassurance that it did not matter who he truly was. Could she still love a man who had gained his current life by taking money for the use of his body?

At last, she spoke. 'You said before that there was a way out of our current predicament,' she said, as if his past did not matter to her. 'What did it have to do with what you just told me?'

'I thought it would be obvious,' he said. 'I have given you all you need to betray me. If you go to Cottsmoor village, you will find someone who can corroborate what I have told you and give you some parts of the story I am honour bound not to divulge. I promise, they are more than enough to shock even the most jaded gossip.'

'And what am I to do with this information once I get it?'

He carefully disengaged himself from her caress, threw back the sheet and swung his legs out of the bed. 'Get the whole truth and bring it back to London. Share the news and ruin me. Your father will be forced to break the engagement immediately and Belle will be free.'

'But what about us?' There was a plaintive note in her voice that told him she had still hoped for a future. But when she sat up, it was on the opposite side of the bed, far from him.

He shook his head, wondering if she could see the denial in the dim light. 'The truth will out and I will not have to break my oath to your father.'

Or to Cottsmoor's family.

The thought actually cheered him for a moment.

'And if I am not worthy of Belle, then I am certainly not worthy of her sister. There is no hope for us, my love.'

'But Belle will be free,' she said hesitantly.

'I will marry her, if that is what you think best. And I will care for her, just as I promised. But you have seen her with me. She does not want this.'

'She does not,' Amy agreed.

'If we truly want what is best for her, we should not force her to accept it. Help me to end this farce of an engagement. Ruin me. But what we have…' He shook his head again. 'It is over, my love. Do what is right, I beg you, no matter how much it hurts.'

Then he left her and walked down the hall to his room.

Chapter Twenty

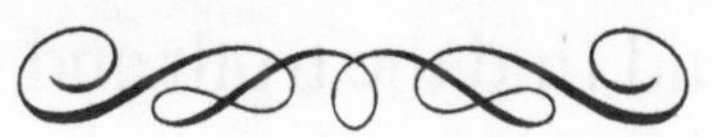

Amy was gone before breakfast had finished, making mock apologies about a sick aunt. She must have explained to her sister, for Belle nodded along with the news as if it was the most natural thing to be left behind in the middle of a family crisis with the man who had walked out on their engagement ball.

He gave her a reassuring smile across the table. 'She will be back soon.'

'Because we do not have an aunt,' Belle said quietly. 'Once she remembers that, she will come back for me.'

'You are probably right. In the meantime, please, make yourself comfortable in my home.' He tried to think of something that might interest her. 'There is a fresh litter of pups in the stables.

I am sure none of them is as nice as Mellie, but they might welcome a visit.'

She smiled and rose from the table. 'I will go see them directly.'

Now there was nothing left for him but the waiting. Amy would find the truth and form her own opinions of it. Then, if she was wise, she would do what he hoped and spread the news about London, bringing a halt to this foolishness.

If she broke the scandal, she would be seen as the brave rescuer of her sister. Belle would have survived a narrow escape from a duplicitous villain and not become the cast-off goods of a gentleman. The result would be the same. But in society, appearances were everything. At the end of the day, Arabella must be blameless.

When he looked up, young Cottsmoor was standing in the doorway of the breakfast room, hands closed into fists and held out before him. Slowly he opened them, revealing the black and white kings of the library chess set. His expression turned hopeful.

Ben pointed to black, as he always did, and smiled back. Then he led the way to the library.

'You will regret giving me the advantage of the first move,' the boy said with a grin, once the door was closed. 'I have been practising since the last time we were together.'

'I am glad to hear it, Your Grace,' he replied. 'If only for the sake of the country. We need clever men to lead us.'

'Thank you, Mr Lovell,' he said and broke out in snorts of laughter. 'Can you not call me John, like you used to?'

Ben smiled. 'It would be a great insult for me to be so informal, Your Grace.'

'I promise not to chop off your head, or whatever I am supposed to do to people who do not behave.' He moved a pawn tentatively forward.

'Ask your uncle. I am sure he will have the answer,' Ben said.

'He would say you should be whipped,' the boy said, sounding slightly worried.

'Because he does not like me,' Ben agreed.

Stay away from the boy. Now that Cassandra is dead, you have no business with the family, you worthless cicisbeo.

Ben's lips thinned in a bitter smile. Dislike was

too mild a word to describe what old Cottsmoor's brother felt for him. But it did not matter. They were only words, after all. He'd heard worse than that from Cassandra, towards the end.

He stared down at the board. It was clear that what had seemed a hesitant beginning had been a ruse to draw his knight. He countered and took a pawn.

'Then I will not tell Uncle when I visit with you. And I insist, as Cottsmoor, that when we are alone, I will be John and you will be Ben, just like it used to be.' The boyish laughter had disappeared and the Duke stared coldly into his eyes, demanding obedience.

'Very well, John,' said Ben with an impressed nod. 'You are becoming quite intimidating.' Though still a cub, he was definitely a lion in the making. And the cub had just taken his bishop.

'In a few years, I will care for nothing and no one,' John answered in a surprisingly adult tone. 'I will think no further than my own pleasure, just like the last Cottsmoor.'

'You will not,' Ben said, in a tone just as imperious as the boy's had been. 'You will think of your

King, your country and the needs of its people. The Dukedom is a reward for the honourable service of the first Cottsmoor. His successors should prove themselves worthy by their actions.'

'That is not what the last Cottsmoor would have said,' John said. 'Not to me, at least. He was too busy doting on the heir.' Anger made John reckless. He had exposed his queen.

Unfortunately, what the boy said was true. The Duke had doted on his first son to the exclusion of everyone else. Though John had been born into the most privileged of lives, the loneliness of his years was still sharp in both their memories. 'Cottsmoor had his reasons.'

John responded with a grim smile, 'And if he can see me now, he regrets them.'

'As do I,' Ben said softly. 'I know how difficult it can be to have no father.' And yet he did not know at all what it must have been like for John. When Ben's own father had died, the loss had nearly crushed him. But it was very different to share a house with one man who refused to acknowledge you existed and another who knew but was forced by circumstances to deny it.

'There was nothing you could have done,' John reminded him.

'I should have found a way,' Ben said. The regret lingered like a bitter aftertaste.

'It was not as if you were allowed in the nursery.'

'It would not have been appropriate,' Ben agreed. Even Cottsmoor's extreme generosity had its limits. They stopped well short of his wife's paramour dandling infants and playing at peekaboo.

'And you did not leave me,' John reminded him.

He had been young and stupid. But he had known in less than a year that his love for Cassandra was a poisonous thing. As more years passed, even his lust had died. And yet he had stayed with her, serviced her, taken her money and hated himself for it. 'I did not leave you,' he said.

John sensed the moment of sentimental weakness and took advantage, moving his bishop to attack. 'Check.'

Ben laughed and gave him a nod of approval before moving a knight to protect his king. 'But you will be a better duke than he was, because of it. Hardship makes you stronger.'

John sighed. 'Sometimes, I wish I did not have to be quite so strong.' Then he moved his queen and smiled again. 'Check.'

Ben moved a rook. 'You might have to be stronger yet. There is something we must discuss.'

'You mean there is something you wish to say that has not been said,' John corrected, taking the rook. 'Check.'

This time, Ben moved his king. 'Sometimes, you are too smart for your own good. In the near future, you will hear unpleasant rumours about me.'

'And I am not to believe them?' the boy said, contemplating the next move.

'On the contrary, they will all be true,' Ben said.

John's eyes widened in surprise. 'What have you done?'

'Nothing recently,' Ben assured him. 'But Summoner knows I am not your brother. He has threatened to reveal it. Miss Amelia Summoner is on her way to Cottsmoor to talk to my mother.'

'I will make them stop,' John said, falling easily into the role of autocrat again. 'Check.'

'Do not bother yourself.' Ben rescued his king yet again. 'I have decided it is better for all concerned if I call his bluff. One cannot blackmail a man who has no secrets.'

'You will be disgraced,' John said, obviously worried. His attention wavered and Ben took his queen on the next move.

'When I am, you must distance yourself from me,' Ben said, though his heart ached at the thought. They'd had precious little time together before Cottsmoor died. Now he would lose the future he had hoped for and any chance to make amends for the past. But there was no alternative. 'I want no stain on your reputation, because of my past behaviour.'

'Do not worry about me,' John said, taking a bishop. 'If Cottsmoor taught me anything, it is that I am far above scandal, even when I am at the centre of it. Pay attention to the game, Ben. Check.'

Ben laughed in surprise and searched the board for his next move. 'I do not know why I worry about you. You have obviously learned to take care of yourself without my help.'

'But I appreciate that you do,' the boy said quietly. 'And I will not allow you to keep your distance to protect me. I have few friends. I cannot afford to lose you.'

'Thank you, John.' He smiled and tipped over his king. 'I see mate in three. An excellent game.'

Pleased, the young Duke nodded. 'Another?'

Ben began to set up the board again. 'You must give me a chance to recover my pride.' As if that was necessary. When he was with the boy, pride seemed to swell inside him like a lump in his throat that sometimes made it difficult to speak. He coughed to clear the roughness from the next words. 'This time, I will take white, since you are near to my equal. But that is no surprise. Your father was an excellent chess player as well.'

'Yes, he is,' John said. 'Yes, he is.'

Chapter Twenty-One

The trip to Cottsmoor took most of the day, what with stops for changes of horses and refreshment. The maid she had brought with her dozed silently in the seat opposite for most of the journey, for she knew well enough not to question the purpose of the trip.

Before she'd left, Amy had gone to her sister's room, shaking her awake. 'Belle. There is something I must tell you.'

The sleepy blonde head rose from the pillow to look at her.

'I need to go somewhere, just for a day or two.'

'You are leaving me alone?' She was instantly awake, staring at Amy in terror.

'Not alone, dear. Your maid will still be with you. And, of course, you can trust Mr Lovell.'

Belle shook her head at this, as though she'd rather do anything in the world other than that.

Amy squeezed her hand. 'Do not be afraid of him. I am going on this journey because he and I discussed your future and how unhappy you are.'

'You told him?' At this, Belle looked even more frightened.

'He understands. And we have found something that will help.'

Belle's eyes went wide. 'Are you going to tell Father? He will be angry.'

'Not yet. When I get back from my trip, in a day, or perhaps two, I will go to him and explain. In the meantime, you must stay here. You must keep my secret until then.'

'A secret?' Belle smiled.

'A good secret.' Amy did her best to smile. 'Now go back to sleep. I will see you again, very soon.'

It had been a lie. There was nothing good about the truths she was going to uncover. What she knew so far was sordid enough. If, as he had hinted, the rest was worse, she did not know if she wanted to hear it.

But the story was fascinating as well. There had been no pride in taking money to do what he had done. But it explained why his current credo was excellence in all things. He had made himself into the man he'd wanted to be and had never looked back.

Now she was entering the sleepy village of Cottsmoor, a place as far as she could imagine from the life that Benjamin Lovell aspired to. It took only a single enquiry at the local inn to learn that Mrs Lovell still lived in a small, rose-covered cottage on the edge of town.

Amy stared out of the carriage window at it, amazed. It was a pleasant little house with a nicely kept garden and a fresh coat of paint on the green front door. Compared to the house she had just left, it seemed so tiny. Though Ben did not spend lavishly, he certainly had the money to spare something for the woman who birthed him.

But neither did it appear that she lived in the poverty he'd hinted at. Perhaps there had been discreet gifts so that she could live in comfort and safety, even though he was not there to care for her.

She got out of the carriage and went up the neatly swept path, then rang the bell and waited.

A maid opened for her, who took only one curious glance at the Summoner carriage before offering refreshment and directing her to sit in the parlour to await the lady of the house.

When she entered the room, Amy had no doubt that she'd found the woman she sought. Though her hair was silver grey, Mrs Lovell had the same high cheekbones and piercing, dark eyes as her son. But there was also the faint cloud of sadness that she sometimes saw when Ben bothered to lower his guard. There was a wistfulness about this woman that spoke to a lost time that could never be regained.

'Miss Summoner?' Mrs Lovell greeted her with courtesy, but was obviously surprised by an unannounced visit from a total stranger.

'Mrs Lovell.' What was one supposed to say at a time like this? And would his mother even welcome the visit? 'I am a friend of your son.' It was not quite true, but it was ever so much easier than the truth.

But it was enough. Before she could say another

word, the woman rushed to her side, reaching to take her hands. 'You know my Benjamin? Do you have word from him? Was there a message?'

The look in response to the slight negative shake of Amy's head was more desperate than she could have imagined.

'It has been so long,' she whispered, closing her eyes, as if in prayer. 'Is he well?'

'He is fine,' Amy added quickly. By the sudden, relieved slump of the older woman's shoulders, it appeared she had been worried that Amy had come to deliver news of his death.

'He is a great man in London. He is welcome in the best homes and has many friends.'

Mrs Lovell squeezed her hands in gratitude, so moved that she could hardly speak. Then she whispered, 'Tell me of him. Tell me everything. When did you see him? How did he look?' She was clearly hungry for any scrap of information.

'I saw him just last night,' she admitted, hoping that her face did not reveal how it had been when they parted. 'It was at a house party in his home in Kew. He is in excellent health, wealthy, well mannered and well respected. He is the most handsome man in London.' And now she had been too effusive in her praise. She wet her lips, embarrassed to go on. 'He is engaged to my sister.'

'Oh.' Mrs Lovell gave her a slow, probing look, as though reassessing everything she had suspected about the visit and Amy's reason for making it. 'But more importantly, is he happy?'

'He's not.' It was the one question she was sure she knew the answer to.

'Oh, dear,' the other woman murmured. 'Oh, dear. I knew, from the first moment that the Duke and his lascivious young wife got their claws in him that it would end in tears.' Mrs Lovell shook her head.

Amy held her hands and led her to sit on the sofa by the fire. 'He has told me only the most basic facts. But he sent me to you to learn the rest.'

'He was a beautiful boy.' She shook her head again. 'He was not even eighteen, when that she-devil first saw him. The Duke was away in London, with friends of his own.' She wrinkled her nose. 'He was no better than his wife and some might say worse.'

'He had mistresses?' Amy said, eyes wide.

The woman nodded. 'And no interest in his duchess after the first boy was born.'

'So she took a lover.'

Mrs Lovell shook her head in regret. 'At first, he would come home from the manor with gold in his pocket and a smile on his face.' Her face contorted with the shame of the memory. 'I took the money he offered. His father died before Ben could learn a trade and left us with nothing. What was I to do?'

'You had no choice,' Amy agreed.

'But then the visits became longer and longer. And when the Duke returned, rather than putting a stop to it, he encouraged it.'

'He befriended him,' Amy said.

'He called him son.' Mrs Lovell's eyes narrowed in loathing. 'Andrew Lovell was a good man. An honest man. When I heard that Ben was claiming that old reprobate as father, I gave him the lecture he deserved. And rather than beg forgiveness for his proud ways, he moved to the great house and did not come back.' By the time she had finished, tears of regret were running down the older woman's face.

'And the Duke allowed him to live there, with his family.' She offered the woman her handkerchief.

'They kept my son like a pet. And when I saw him after that, he was riding through the village in the Duke's carriage, dressed like a gentleman. Or side by side on horseback with that red-headed succubus of a duchess, talking French and laughing at her jokes.' She gave a shudder of distaste. 'No matter how hard he laughed, I could see he was not happy. But when he saw me…' She flinched again. 'He looked right through me.'

'And he did not come home, even after the old Duke died?' He must have known how he'd hurt her. How could he have left his mother to suffer?

She shook her head. 'By then, it was too late. After what they gave him, he was too good to come home to me.'

'I am sure it was not that,' Amy said and paused, remembering the bleakness in his voice as he had told her his story. 'I think he was ashamed.'

'I would have forgiven him for what he had

done,' Mrs Lovell said, her lip trembling. 'And I did not care what people might say, when they saw us together.'

'What did they say to you?'

'If they thought he was Cottsmoor's son, then I must have been his whore.'

It was true. While society might forgive a man his natural birth, it was seldom so charitable to the women who bore the bastards. 'Surely, after all this time, the scandal is old news,' she said. Perhaps in this village. But when she told it in London, it would be a nine-days' wonder.

'It has been more than fifteen years.' Mrs Lovell nodded. 'Both the Duke and Duchess are gone to judgement and cannot hurt him, or anyone else, ever again.'

'And their son,' Amy agreed. Then she paused, adding the years in her head. 'You say it has been fifteen years?'

'Or more,' Mrs Lovell replied. 'Would you like to see a picture of my boy? The Duchess had a miniature painted of him shortly after he went to her.' She made a face at the mention of the other woman, but smiled as she reached for the chain around her neck to unfasten it.

'When she died, he mailed it to me.' Now the woman who had raised him lifted her head in defiance. 'He sent me money as well. More than I would ever need. I do not spend it. I do not want money. All I want is to see him once more and to hear from his own lips that he is well.' She shook her head and released a watery sigh as she handed Amy the locket.

She opened it to see just what she had known would be there. At first glance, she would have assumed it was a painting of the young Duke of Cottsmoor. But a closer look proved the young man in the miniature was three or four years older than the Duke. The painter had managed to capture the distant look in the eyes of this boy that she saw in her own beloved Ben.

He had said there were secrets that he was bound by honour not to tell. This was surely what he meant. But was it a secret if the world knew but refused to believe? It did not matter who Cottsmoor's true father might be. The acknowledged son of a duke was the Duke's son, and therefore also a duke. But the embarrassment of rumour might be enough to separate Ben from his young friend for good.

If he lost a son because of her, he could regain a mother. 'He is still just as handsome as this.' Amy handed her the locket back. 'Would you like to see him?'

The older woman stared hungrily down at the picture in her hand as if wishing would bring him live to her doorstep. 'There would be no sweeter gift than to have my boy back,' Mrs Lovell murmured. 'Even if it is only for a little while.'

'Suppose I could give you that?' Amy said, feeling half-hopeful, half-guilty. 'I will take you to him, this very day, if that is what you wish.'

'Please,' the woman said, squeezing the locket tight in her hand.

'We will go as soon as you are ready. But you must do me one favour in return.' Amy held her breath, hating what she was about to do.

'Anything.' Mrs Lovell leaned forward in her chair as if ready to leave with just the clothes on her back.

'When we arrive in London, you must tell my

father the story you have just told me. Immediately after, I will take you to Ben. And then he will take you home.' He would have to, for it would be too humiliating to remain in London. Would the woman beside her still be so eager to go if she knew that their visit might be the first step in ruining her son's life?

Chapter Twenty-Two

Now that there was nothing to do but wait for his plan to come to fruition, the hours seemed to drag so slowly that the clock might have been standing still. Although what he was waiting for, he was not sure.

It was unlikely that he would hear anything at all until he returned to London at the end of the week. It would take a day for Amy to reach Cottsmoor and another to return to London. Once there, she would learn that her father knew the truth and was not planning to use it. She would have to find another way.

She was sensible enough to take the story to the person who could do the most damage with it. A patroness at Almack's would be an excellent choice. Soon, there would be one of those horrible stories in the papers about Mr L., the late Duchess of C. and the broken heart of the beautiful Miss S. In no time at all, the Summoner family would close ranks against him, and the rest of the *ton* would cast him out.

Was it really so wrong of him to hope that, once she had learned the whole sordid story, Amy would love him enough to follow him into exile? It was doubtful that she would come back to the man who had supposedly broken Belle's heart. Her first concern had always been for her sister.

No matter what might transpire, he would be the one to hurt her. He was doing the best thing for Belle, just as he had promised. There was nothing left to do but wait for the inevitable.

Thank God, there were no activities planned for the guests today. After his spectacular failure as host on the previous evening, he was at a loss as to how he might recover the goodwill of his friends. In fact, all of them save John could go to the devil. Since John had gone riding after beating him three times at the chessboard, Ben wanted nothing more than an afternoon of solitude.

Perhaps there was a book in the library that

was not too melancholy and could fill the last few hours before dinner.

As he opened the door to the room there was a sudden rustling, as though it had taken a flurry of activity to change whatever had been going on into a scene acceptable to prying eyes. Which made him wonder just what he had interrupted, for Guy Templeton was seated on the leather sofa far too close to his fiancée, holding both of her hands in his. The tails of his cravat hung loose down the front of his waistcoat.

Belle's gown and hair were dishevelled and her cheeks were flushed, but it was hard to tell if it was from passion, or simply because she was weeping, openly, loudly and in a most unattractive and unladylike way.

'Templeton? Explain yourself.' Ben squared his shoulders, hoping he would not have to challenge his friend because of an unsatisfactory answer. It was even more annoying that his own anger at this scene was little more than a gentlemanly reflex and had nothing to do with any possessive affection for Belle.

'What have *I* done?' Guy looked at him with a

frown and raised eyebrow, as if it was possible to lay the tragedy, whatever it was, at Ben's doorstep.

'He wants to go away,' Belle said, with another sob.

Templeton put a consoling hand on her shoulder and glared defiantly back at Ben as if daring him to demand its removal.

'Back home?' Ben said, surprised by her reaction. 'It is hardly the end of the world. He lives less than a mile from here. When you come to live with me, we will visit him often.' Not that it was likely she would be here, once Amy had finished with him.

'Actually, I was thinking of something a bit further away,' Templeton said calmly. 'I have been trying to explain to Belle that Virginia is not something that one can come and go from like taking the mail coach to Bath.'

Now it was Ben who was shocked. 'Are you mad? We are at war.'

'And they are likely in need of soldiers for it,' Templeton said with finality.

'You mean to buy a commission?'

'If that is what is necessary. The alternative is

that she comes away with me to Gretna Green, immediately. But we have not got that far in the discussion because I made her cry with my other plan.' Templeton seemed more frustrated with his own ineptitude than the girl's lack of understanding.

But Belle brightened immediately at being presented with an alternative. 'Then I will go to the Green place with you. Why are we going there?'

'So he can marry you,' Ben said, calmly.

She smiled in relief. 'I would rather marry you than Mr Lovell. Let us go right now, before Amy comes back to stop me.' It did not seem to occur to her that Ben might have reason to stop the elopement, as well.

'I do not know if you can marry me, now that Ben has heard our plans,' Templeton explained gently. 'Our going to Gretna was to be a surprise for him.'

'I'm sorry if I spoiled it,' Belle said, looking truly contrite.

'Do not worry,' Ben assured her. 'I am definitely surprised.' He looked back at Templeton. 'How well do you know Miss Arabella?'

'Well enough that she should not marry anyone but me,' Templeton said, not the least bit contrite. 'We were alone at Vauxhall for quite some time.'

'You did not...'

'I was on my way to offer for her when you delivered your good news on Bond Street.' His friend gave a disgusted shake of his head.

'You should have said something,' Ben replied.

'And you could have noticed the obvious,' Templeton retorted. 'I've spent every spare minute with her since the beginning of the Season. I did not want to state my intentions until I was sure she understood the implications of them. I love her with my whole heart, but I did not wish to rush her into something she did not want.'

'As I did,' Ben said, ashamed.

'But then, when we were alone...'

'Things got out of hand,' Ben finished for him. 'I can understand how that might have happened.'

Templeton nodded. 'I suspect, by your lack of anger with me, that Miss Amelia was in the vicinity when you learned the lesson.'

'We are not talking of me and Amy. This conversation is about you and my fiancée.'

'That is correct,' Templeton replied. 'With her sister gone from the house, I meant to act quickly and convince Miss Summoner to run away with me.'

'I suppose I should be trying to stop you,' Ben said. 'And I will, if the lady is not willing.' He sat down in the chair opposite them. 'Now it is your turn to talk, Belle. Your father wants you to marry me. But he and I should not be the ones to decide. Who would you like to marry?'

Belle bit her lip, as if the mention of her father made her afraid to answer.

'It is all right,' Ben assured her. 'I promised your father on the Bible that I would take care of you and make sure you were always happy. Who makes you happiest?'

She looked immediately to Templeton. 'I told Amy that I did not want to marry you. I wanted to marry Guy. She said I could not, because he had not asked.' She gave him a hesitant smile. 'And I do not want him to go away. I would be very unhappy if I could not see him any more.'

He looked to Templeton. 'You understand her difficulties and are not concerned with them?'

'She needs patience. Nothing more than that.' Templeton shrugged. 'And I do not claim to be the cleverest man in London as you do. I am happy with her, just as she is.'

Guy smiled at Belle and touched the tip of her nose, making her giggle. 'More than content, actually. I am hopelessly in love with you.'

Ben cleared his throat to remind them that they were not alone. 'I think what I am supposed to do at this juncture is to call you out and put a sword through you.'

'You can try,' Templeton replied. 'But I would rather you didn't.'

Belle reached out to grab his hand and put her body in front of his, to shield him. Then she gave Ben a militant glare that was every bit as pretty as her smile.

He sighed. 'It is a good thing for all of us that I swore to Summoner that I would do what was best and make his daughter happy. I cannot do either of those things by marrying her.' He raised his hands in surrender.

'We have your blessing, then?' Templeton put

his hands on Belle's shoulders and pulled her back to his side.

'You do if you go quickly,' Ben said. 'I will give you several hours' head start before I find the note you will be leaving me. I will be too distraught to go immediately to Summoner and will search without success. But her father will have to be told, eventually.'

'There will be a scandal, of course,' Templeton said.

'Surprisingly, not as big a scandal as I was expecting,' Ben said, trying not to smile. 'But the important thing is that Miss Arabella has the husband she really wants.'

Belle smiled at him with the mind-melting brilliance that had attracted all the men in London. 'Mellie is right. You are a nice man. But I am glad I do not have to marry you.'

'And I am glad I do not have to marry you,' Ben admitted. Then he leaned forward to kiss her on the cheek. 'We can be neighbours instead,' he said.

'That will be nice,' she said.

Templeton rose and offered her his hand, pulling her after. 'It is all settled then. Give my apologies to Miss Amelia when you see her next.'

'I will do that,' he said, wondering if, after Summoner heard the news, he would be allowed to see either of the girls ever again.

Chapter Twenty-Three

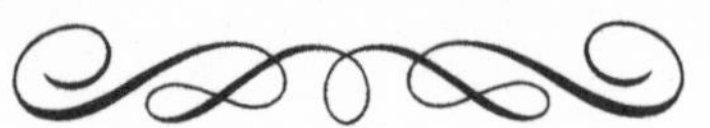

Pushing the horses to their limit and travelling through the night, Amy and Mrs Lovell arrived back in London little more than a day from the time she had left Ben's house. If the older woman had questions about the need to speak to Amy's father before visiting Ben, she did not ask them. To her, it was but a small obstacle on the trip she had been longing to make.

Only Amy questioned the wisdom of the trip. Suppose her father humiliated the woman with questions about her virtue or tried to pay her to make the truth go away?

As if sensing her worries, Mrs Lovell laid a hand on hers. 'This must be awful for you, my dear. When scandal rears its head, it is difficult to look the beast in the eye. But you must trust me. No matter what is about to happen, it will be better for all involved than doing nothing. Our secrets have been bottled up for far too long.' She finished with an encouraging smile.

Amy took a deep breath and answered with a smile of her own. Then she ushered the woman into the Summoner town house and made her comfortable in the receiving room before she went to seek out her father.

As usual, he was in his office when she rushed in without introduction, fearing that delay might make her lose her nerve. 'Father—' she leaned over the desk to confront him '—you must end Belle's engagement immediately! I have discovered the unfortunate truth about Mr Lovell. It is all quite shocking. There is a woman here you must speak to, who can verify all I have learned.'

Her father stared across the desk at her, simmering with annoyance. 'Whatever this woman has to say should remain between her and Mr Lovell, Amelia. It is no longer any concern of ours.'

'No concern of ours? Of course it concerns us. He is to marry Belle. She will be ruined.'

'She is ruined already and by her own hand,'

Lord Summoner said with a disgusted sigh. 'And nothing would have happened if you had not failed in the one task you were entrusted with. Instead of watching over her, you left your sister alone to go chasing stories that I knew long before I spoke to Mr Lovell.'

'You knew?' It explained why Ben had been unwilling to break the engagement himself. Her father had been using his past against him.

'What I knew is immaterial. What I *did not know* was that your sister would take your unplanned absence as an excuse to elope.'

Amy sat down hard in the chair in front of the desk, suddenly at a loss. When she could manage to speak, she asked, 'With whom?'

'Guy Templeton. The very man whose case you were pleading the day I promised Belle to Lovell.' Her father's eyes narrowed. 'Did you orchestrate this disobedience? Because if you knew and arranged this trip simply so you would not be blamed…'

'What utter nonsense. You know, Father, that if I meant to disobey you, there would have been no subterfuge involved.'

'I suppose that is true,' he said, after a moment's thought. 'You really are the most contrary creature.'

'And I did know that Templeton was fond of her,' Amy admitted. 'But since the engagement, I have been doing my best to warn her off him. I had no idea that things had progressed so far.'

But she had. Belle had all but admitted the truth to her, and argued for her right to think independently and marry the man she loved. In return she had scolded her and told her the exact thing that everyone else did: that she was not smart enough to know her own mind on the most important decision of her life.

And now Amy did not know whether to be hopeful for Belle or horrified. But she definitely felt ashamed of her own behaviour. 'Is there no chance we can get her to come back?'

Her father shook his head. 'Their absence was not noted for some time. Lovell found a note, explaining their intentions. I suppose we must console ourselves that he means to marry her.'

'Oh.' In either case, Belle had likely spent more than one night as a woman with no feminine instruction and with only Guy Templeton for company. Surprisingly, the thought did not panic her as it should have. Instead, it seemed more than right. She had a gentle and caring husband to teach her what she needed to know.

Most of her recent advice to her sister had been totally wrong, anyway. Perhaps in this, it would be better to let Belle make her own way. 'I am sure Mr Templeton loves her, Father. And she is very fond of him as well. It will be all right.' Having seen the look in Mr Templeton's eyes as they'd danced, it was obvious that they belonged together, no matter what others might think. Wherever they were now, they were probably quite happy.

'But I do not want Guy Templeton as a son,' her father shouted. 'The man is a ninny. Even worse than that, he is a Whig.' At this, he held his head in his hands, clearly beyond consolation. 'Lovell sent a search party after them, as soon as he knew, but they were too quick. He blames himself, since he was the one who invited that damned interloper into his home. But really, it was all your fault.' He glared at Amy again. 'If you had left well enough alone and watched your sister instead of abandoning her to search for things that did not concern you, this never would have happened.'

Leaving Kew was far from her greatest sin of the week. But if it made her father feel better to blame her, she would allow it, if only so she didn't have to explain herself. 'I am sure Mr Lovell will recover,' she said, trying not to smile.

'Thank you so much for your opinion, Amelia,' he said, sarcastically. 'But suppose he doesn't? What am I to do to make amends? I promised the man a future in government and the hand of my daughter. I have no idea what to say to him, now.'

'You still have the seats to offer,' she reminded him. 'And you have two daughters.' She regretted the words as soon as they were out of her mouth.

'It is not as if I need to be reminded of the fact. You are standing right in front of me.' By the look on his face, the information was currently an unpleasant truth. 'But we live in modern England and not the Book of Genesis. I cannot exactly throw a veil over you and trade one girl for another like Leban tricked Jacob.'

'You are probably right,' she said with a moue of feigned disappointment. 'Especially since it was your trickery over Belle's engagement that has brought us to this point. I doubt he will trust anything you say, should you try to hand him me as a substitute.'

'Do not be flippant with me, girl.'

In the past, she might have let the comment pass unremarked. Today, she was in no mood to be bullied. 'Do not be flippant. Is that what you said to Belle that left her crying on the day we departed for Kew? She told us both that she did not want to marry him. We have got what we deserved for ignoring her.'

'All I wanted was for her to be safely married,' he snapped back. 'It was my perfectly reasonable hope that one of my daughters would obey me.'

'I will go to him immediately and offer apologies,' she said. And congratulations as well. His reputation had not suffered the blow they'd both expected. 'Where might I find him?'

Her father laughed. 'Am I his keeper? He is

not here, if that is what you are wondering. Why would he be? I suspect he has gone back to his rooms to drown his sorrows. The loss of a fiancée to a man who claimed to be his friend was terribly embarrassing, no matter how gracious he pretended to be about it.'

When she collected Mrs Lovell from the receiving room, she could but hope that their raised voices had not carried down the hall from the office. If the older woman guessed any of what had transpired, she gave no sign of it. Nor was she particularly bothered by the fact that they were to go immediately back to the carriage.

When Amy informed her that their next stop was to be the address on Bond Street where her son might be found, she tensed slightly, as if suddenly afraid to do the very thing she had wanted all along. 'Does he expect us?' she asked in a quiet voice.

Amy shook her head. 'But we will not be the first unexpected thing to happen to him this week.' And, even after her father's dire rant on the subject, there was no reason to expect that they would be unwelcome.

They arrived at the building and climbed the stairs to his rooms. There, they were greeted at the door by a manservant who directed them to a small parlour overlooking the street. Mrs Lovell was so fascinated by the crowds of people on the street below them that she did not notice the arrival of her son.

Ben stood in the doorway, staring at the woman on the sofa as if he could not quite believe what he was seeing. Amy waited in silence to see his reaction. Though he had given her the facts she needed to bring this reunion about, he had not requested that she return with his mother and risk tarring her with the brush of scandal.

The lady shifted in her seat, turning to face the door at the sound of his gasp.

'Mother.' For a moment, the reserved façade disappeared and he looked like the young Cottsmoor. He had become a boy again, his desire for independence at war with the urge to return to the comfort of his mother's embrace. Then the Benjamin Lovell she knew returned and he strode forward, pulling the woman out of her chair and enveloping her in his arms, pressing his dry cheek to her wet one, offering comfort instead of taking it.

As he hugged her, his features contorted in pain. Then the expression faded and he was at peace, his eyes closed tight, as if trying to freeze the moment and keep it for ever in memory.

'Benjamin,' his mother sobbed. 'It has been so long.'

'I am so sorry,' he whispered back. 'Sorry for what I said, when we argued. When I left you, I did not think it would be forever. But there was a reason I could not leave.'

'The Duchess,' she said, making a face.

'No.' He leaned close to whisper in his mother's ear.

Her face relaxed in an understanding smile. 'It is hard for a boy to become a man without a father to teach him.'

'A boy needs both his parents,' he said, in a ragged voice. 'A mother and a father. I never should have left you.'

'It is all right,' she said, patting his hand. 'And look at you now.' She held him away from her to admire him. 'Tall and handsome. Wealthy and educated. That is what a mother wants for her son, to see him do well.'

'But I left you behind,' he said, sounding again like the boy she had lost. 'And the things I did to make my future…I am no longer worthy to be your son.'

Amy bit her lip to keep from speaking. He had become so much more than he had been. But, even though he had reconciled with his mother, there were still so many things he could never admit to the world.

'It is all in the past,' Mrs Lovell said in a soothing voice. 'If there is a penance, by now you have paid it tenfold. Forgive yourself as I forgave you, years ago.' Then she kissed him upon the forehead as one might when putting a child to sleep.

His shoulders slumped, but it was in acceptance, not defeat. Then he straightened again, and he seemed even taller than he had been, as if the shame that had weighted him down was gone. When he turned back to Amy, he looked different, as well. The grim determination behind his smile was gone, replaced by a lightness of spirit that she had not seen in him before.

She wanted to go to him, to have him hold her and tell her that his mind was as free as his heart. She wanted to know that he loved her and wanted her, just as he had claimed to before. But now he needed to be with the woman he loved, but hadn't seen in years.

Amy rose to excuse herself. 'You must have much to talk about.' As she turned to go, she kept her eyes downcast, not wanting him to see her longing for reassurance.

'Wait.' He leaned forward to whisper into his mother's ear again and Amy saw her smile. Then he rose. 'Let me escort you out, Miss Summoner.'

She responded with a nod of thanks and an attempt at a smile to hide her disappointment. Was she to be Miss Summoner again?

He laid a hand on her shoulder, shepherding her to the door. 'Thank you.' His voice was warm, friendly. But there was no trace of the passion she had heard in it when last they'd parted.

'I didn't do it to help you,' she reminded him.

'I know. But the reason does not matter. It is the good that that has come from your actions. I, of all people, must believe that. All that has happened has happened for the best.'

'But your son,' she whispered. 'Without knowing, my father might have announced the truth to the world.'

'I have no son,' Ben said, the regret returning to his eyes. 'Cottsmoor did. When he claimed him, I lost all right.'

'But to live a lie…' she said, shaking her head.

'As you did for your sister,' he reminded her. 'It was shared guilt that drew us together.'

'I have no regret,' she insisted.

'But perhaps you should,' he whispered. 'You know now who I really am.' He shook his head in amazement. 'I am sorry for the burden of secrecy I have placed on you, even if it is to one other person. I cannot explain what a gift that it is to have told the truth.'

Words of gratitude were sweet. But they were not what she was seeking from him. Where was the love he'd whispered about in the dark?

Perhaps, as she had always thought, the word

meant something different to a man. Perhaps she had misunderstood. Or perhaps she had given him something today that he wanted more than he could ever want her: confession, forgiveness and absolution.

'If it has made you happy, then I am happy,' she said. She loved him. And she had learned from loving Belle that sometimes love meant you wanted the best for your beloved, even if it destroyed your own dreams.

They were at the door now. Only a few more steps until he allowed her to walk away. He paused and she held her breath, waiting for the word that would make her stay.

Instead, he said nothing, and looked both ways to make sure they were not seen before he leaned forward to kiss her on the forehead in a way that was more brotherly than passionate. 'We will see each other soon. Until then, thank you.' He pressed her hand with his to emphasise the depths of his emotion. And then he waited for her to pass through the door so he could close it behind her.

Chapter Twenty-Four

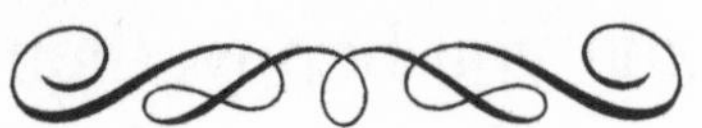

It was another painfully ordinary afternoon in the Summoner home, but with a few major changes. Belle Templeton was visiting her sister and had settled in her usual seat beside the window to make a hash of a lace-trimmed pillow slip. Amy was in her usual seat on the opposite side of the window, ready to rip out the stitches again when it all went horribly wrong.

'I like sewing now,' Belle said with a ladylike nod.

'You do?' Amy looked up in surprise.

'It is a thing that married ladies should like to do,' Belle said. 'So I like it now.' She handed the project to Amy for inspection.

Marriage had not improved her technique in the least. But at least she enjoyed the attempt more than she had in the past. Amy gave her a nod of approval. 'You are trying very hard to be a good wife, aren't you?'

'Guy says I am doing a wonderful job.' Belle leaned forward and whispered, 'There are things that married ladies do that are much easier than sewing and much more fun.'

'That's nice,' said Amy, faintly. 'But I am sure your husband would not want you talking about them.'

'He said I was not to tell you about that time in Vauxhall Gardens,' she said. 'But I am sure, now that I am married it is all right.'

Amy blinked in shock and focused on the needlework in her lap like the proper spinster she'd always claimed she wanted to be. At the back of her mind, she must have known that one day, Belle would outstrip her in knowledge of some subject. Since Belle was to be the one to marry, it was only logical that it would be this one.

There was something deeply consoling about needlework. If one did not care about the results, one did not even have to think while doing the task. At some point, she would look back on today's stitching and notice the unevenness of it. Then she could pull it out and do it again.

But it was no longer necessary to care so much about her work, or Belle's. From the besotted look on Mr Templeton's face when he came to collect her after her visits with Amy, the last thing in the world he cared about was whether his wife could stitch a straight seam.

When she had hinted to him about Belle's need for assistance in the running of the house, he had politely but firmly refused her offer of help. Worse yet, Belle, who had been so dependent on her before, showed no interest in opening her home to Amelia the spinster. Apparently, the happy couple had not forgotten her efforts to keep them apart and no longer required her assistance.

Her sister was happy. That was what she'd wanted, all along. But she had never imagined a future where her own life had passed by unlived while she managed Belle's. And now, without her quiet sister in it, the house was emptier than she could have imagined.

When she glanced up from her work to check on her sister, Belle was staring back at her. 'Are you sad?' She put aside her work basket and leaned forward to lay a hand on Amy's cheek.

Amy forced a smile. 'Do not worry yourself. I am fine.' Belle was happy. She reminded herself of that fact several times a day. She had always told herself that this would be enough. And now to pretend that it was so made her throat tighten.

'Do you want to come with Mary and me to pick curtains for my new house? I think I like blue. Guy says I can have any colour I want.'

'But not white,' Amy said, smiling. 'You are very lucky to have found a man as good to you as Guy.' Then she paused, repeating her sister's last words in her mind. 'Who is Mary?'

'Mary is my new friend. Mr Lovell says she is coming to live with us and help me with the things I do not know about running a house and being a wife. That way, you do not have to.'

'But…' She wanted to live with Belle. It was not a burden. And what else was she to do?

Belle's smile had not dimmed. 'I like Mary. She is very nice.'

'You've met her?'

Belle nodded happily. 'She likes me, too.'

She had been replaced. Amy took a moment to control her temper before speaking. There was no point in being angry with Belle. She could not have known what the news would mean, if Amy had not known it herself until just that moment. 'Of course she likes you,' she said, not losing the smile. 'And I am glad you are happy. Truly, I am.'

'At first, when you said I had to get married and leave home, I was frightened,' Belle said. 'But it is very nice. I like being married. You should do it, too.'

Amy swallowed until she could breathe around the lump in her throat. She had not seen Ben at all since the day she had brought his mother to him. It had been almost a week and there had been no visit, no letter, nor any sign of him at the parties she'd attended. If he felt any of the things he'd claimed to, what had become of him?

It took almost a minute to remember that she had decided years ago that she did not want to get married and was happy with things just the way they were. 'I am far too old to marry,' she said, forcing her smile to be as bright as Belle's. 'And Father still needs me. I shall remain here and take care of him.' Not that Geoffrey Summoner needed caring for. She had never met a more independent man in her life. 'Perhaps I will get a cottage near Mr Templeton's home so I can come to your house in the afternoons, as you do to mine. Then I might help with the mending and other things you do not like.' But the thought of a lifetime spent re-stitching Belle's spoiled hems made her want to weep.

Her plans had not been as noble and selfless as she had thought them. She had assumed that she would simply follow Belle in marriage. She had wanted to arrange a future that would suit her own needs as much as her sister's. But she had forgotten that even a man as gentle and kind as Guy Templeton might not want to share his life with a sister-in-law who could not be bothered to find a husband.

'I will have Mary and Guy for things like that.' Belle was glancing out the window of the sitting room towards the street in front of the house. Then she leaned forward in her chair, too excited to be still. 'He is here! He has come to take me home.' Now her face lit with a smile that was different from the one she used to wear. There was a warmth and depth to it that had been missing from her childlike joy for parties and dancing.

Belle was in love.

Before she could stifle it, a sob escaped from Amy's lips. It was just as Ben had always claimed. She was jealous of her sister. And she was angry at the fact that she had given so much and, in the end, there was nothing left for her. She had no love of her own and her sister did not need her.

'Don't be sad.' Belle's hand was on her cheek again, her husband's arrival forgotten. 'Guy promises that he will take good care of me.'

Who will take care of me?

Of course, she did not need anyone to take care of her. She was quite capable of making her own decisions and managing her own life. But at a moment like this, she could not help but wonder if it might be nicer not to be so completely independent.

'I will miss you,' she whispered, cupping Belle's face in her palms.

'You do not have to miss me. We can be neighbours.' Belle beamed at her again. 'You must marry Mr Lovell. Guy says he lives so close we can walk there.'

'But...' Was it really necessary to explain, again, that a woman had no power in this? 'I cannot just decide to marry Mr Lovell. He must ask me. And there is no reason for him to do so.' None that she could admit to, anyway. Without thinking, she touched the locket that hung at her throat.

'I know something you don't know.' Belle was trying to look smug as a kitten in the cream. But since she could not manage to stop giggling, the effect was spoiled.

'Not about this, I'm afraid.' Amy pulled Belle's hand from her face, clasping it in her own.

'I know that you like Mr Lovell, even though you pretend that you do not.'

What point was there to lie about it now? 'Yes, I do.'

'And he likes you, too. That is why he's talking to Papa.'

'He's talking...' She paused in confusion. 'When did he talk to Father?'

'He is talking to him right now,' Belle said. 'I saw him come in.'

'You saw him?'

'I have been watching out the window for Guy,' she said. 'And when I saw him on the street…' she pointed towards the front door '…he saw me in the window, and he…' She held her finger up to her lips to indicate silence.

Amy shook her head. Belle was not making much sense. But then, she often got more confusing when there was something important to convey. 'Mr Lovell wanted you to keep his visit a secret?'

Belle frowned. 'Did I do wrong?'

'No,' Amy assured her. 'I am sure he just wished to surprise me.' It was far more likely that he had business with her father and hoped to save them both the embarrassment of a meeting. If he left the house as quietly as he arrived she need never know he had been there.

Belle had no intention of allowing discretion. She stood and tugged on Amy's hand to pull her to her feet. 'You should go to him.'

'No, Belle,' she said quietly. 'I am sure, if he wants to see me, he will come.'

'She is right, Belle. Ben must come to her.' Guy

Templeton was standing in the doorway, with Mellie the terrier pulling on the leash in his hand. He dropped the leather strap and the dog ran past his mistress to throw himself on to his favourite spot on the sofa.

'Guy.' Belle dropped her sister's hands and went to her husband, pulling him into the room.

'My angel,' he said, giving her a kiss on the cheek. 'How was your afternoon?'

'I made a pillowslip,' she said. 'It is very bad.'

He looked down at it. 'It is.' Then he whispered something in her ear that made her laugh.

'Templeton.' Their father was standing in the doorway Guy had vacated. He was glaring at his new son-in-law with an expression of thinly veiled contempt.

'Lord Summoner.' Guy looked back at him with a serene smile devoid of offence. He took a step closer to Belle in a subtle display of possession. 'I have come to collect my wife.'

At the last word, Father gave a visible wince of displeasure. 'Then do so and be gone.' He looked at Belle, his gaze softening. 'And if you need to return home, for any reason, you are not to hesitate. I will send a carriage immediately.'

At this, Belle laughed. 'Do not be silly, Papa. If I wish to come here, Guy will drive me in his own carriage. And then he will come to bring me home, just as he is doing now.'

For a moment, their father had the same perplexed look on his face that summed up what she felt about her sister's new-found independence. He gave one more cold glance in Guy's direction and said, 'Very well, then.'

'Very well,' Belle agreed. 'Come, Mellie. We are leaving now.' Guy offered her his arm and escorted her towards the door. But as she passed her father in the doorway, she stopped to kiss him on the cheek.

For a moment, he softened and his hand rose, as if to beckon her back. Then it dropped again and he sighed in defeat.

Mellie sighed as well, hopping to the floor and giving one last, longing look at his cushion before wagging his tail and following his mistress out of the house.

Her father cleared his throat, as if coughing

away the inconveniently soft emotions. 'Amelia. I wish to see you in my study.'

She gathered up her sewing. 'I will be with you momentarily.'

'Now, Amelia. We do not want to keep our guest waiting.'

Ben.

She had assumed he must be gone. But he was in this very house with her, waiting. She stood up so quickly she dropped her workbasket and smoothed her skirts and hair, wishing for a mirror. Then she did her best to walk at a ladylike pace one step behind her father.

But she touched the locket for luck as she did so.

As she entered the room, he rose, turned and bowed. But his face remained expressionless, giving no hint of what was to come. He waited until she had taken the chair on the opposite end of the desk before resuming his seat.

She looked from one to the other, but neither man spoke. The silence drew her nerves to the breaking point, so, she broke it. 'Good afternoon, Mr Lovell. What business did you have with me?'

He showed no mercy and did not answer the

question she had asked. 'I came to assure myself that your sister was well and offer my apologies again for what happened in my home.'

'No apologies are necessary,' her father said hurriedly.

Ben held up a hand to demur. 'Despite my efforts to do just as your father wished, my engagement to your sister ended badly. I promised that she would not be hurt and wished to assure myself that all was well with her.'

'I assume you know it to be so,' Amy said, growing impatient. 'For it appears you helped her husband to engage a companion for her.'

'How gracious of you,' her father said, smiling.

'So kind,' she added, 'to make it unnecessary for me to follow her to her new home.'

'It was the least I could do,' Ben said, ignoring the warning glare her father shot her and responding with a modest nod. 'I wanted to be sure my oath to you was properly discharged.'

'Of course, my dear fellow. Any obligation is fulfilled. You have done all you could.'

'But that still leaves the matter of the seat in the

Commons we discussed,' Ben added. 'And certain threats that you made against my character.'

'They were not meant as threats, per se,' her father hedged.

'I spoke to Cottsmoor about them. He found them to be most ominous.'

'Cottsmoor?' her father said weakly.

'I believe you said something about biblical retribution, if I failed in my duty,' Ben said quietly.

'Father is a great fan of the Bible,' Amy supplied. 'Especially Genesis. Jacob and Esau. Leban and Rachel…' She gave him a significant look and pretended to veil her face.

'And you did not fail, Mr Lovell,' her father said, ignoring her. 'I have no reason to seek retribution.'

'But that does not reduce the power you have over me,' Ben reminded him, turning to her. 'And you as well, Miss Summoner. For you took the time to find my mother and verify the truth about my past.'

At your request.

She wanted to shout it at him and end this pointless charade.

'I am sure she meant no harm,' her father wheedled.

'On the contrary, she has been trying to harm me since the first day we met,' Ben said with a laugh of incredulity. 'Spilling drinks. Knocking me off a horse. And locking me in a closet at the Middletons' musicale.'

'That door was not locked,' she insisted, before remembering where she was.

'Amelia!' her father said, obviously appalled.

'In short, I have no reason to trust the pair of you,' Ben finished.

'No more than I trust you,' she said, growing tired of waiting for him to make good on his words.

'But there is no need to involve a peer,' her father said hastily. 'I am sure we can come to a mutually agreeable resolution.'

'I would have more faith in your words if you had as much to lose as I,' Ben reminded him. 'If we were related, by a bond of marriage, as planned? Then the last thing you would want was to see me disgraced.'

The room fell silent and both men looked to her.

'It was never my intention to marry,' she said to her father, trying not to smile at his suffering.

'And I promised that I would not force a husband upon you,' he replied. 'But for all that is holy, just once would you consider doing what is best for both of us?'

She sighed. 'This is not much of a proposal. You did better by my sister, I think. She at least got a carriage ride.'

'After the preliminaries were settled in this office,' Ben responded. 'And I have not, as yet, proposed to you. You cannot complain about my technique until after.'

'You have my permission and she has not rejected you on principal,' her father said, throwing up his hands. 'You have already got further with her than any other man.'

Ben's next comment was lost in an embarrassed cough. He cleared his throat again and her father reached for the brandy, pouring them both a glass and ignoring Amy's outstretched hand.

'As I was about to say…' Ben glanced in her direction with a polite smile and drained his glass.

'If the lady and I can speak privately for a time, perhaps we can come to an understanding.'

'By all means,' her father said. 'Go to the sitting room and talk for as long as you like.'

Ben rose and preceded her.

When he was out of earshot, her father said in an angry whisper, 'And do not come out of that room until you have said yes. I will lock you in together, if I must. But there will be a marriage and the matter will be settled.'

'I will consider his offer,' she said, trying not to laugh. Then she swept out of the office with the imperious glare of a disapproving spinster. She walked down the hall to the room where her lover waited and shut the door behind them, turning the key in the lock.

He glanced at the handle. 'Are you sure that is wise?'

'It was recommended to me,' she assured him. 'Either we lock it, or he will do it for us.'

'It is always a comfort to have the support of the father when making an offer,' he said, drily.

'It is also necessary to have the support of the woman you wish to marry,' she reminded him.

He hesitated. 'Once, not long ago, I thought I had it. But if, after you know the truth about me, you have changed your mind, tell me now. I will go immediately and speak no more about this.'

'Do not be foolish,' she said, stepping into his arms. 'As your mother said, it was very long ago.'

'And I was very young,' he said, by way of explanation. 'And I thought I was in love.'

'Did she love you in return?'

He rested his chin on the top of her head, holding her close. 'For a time, perhaps. But neither she nor her husband were capable of really loving anyone but themselves.'

'But what of your son?' she pressed, and felt him still.

The look in his eyes grew distant. 'I am honoured to be a friend of the Duke of Cottsmoor,' he said. 'He is a fine boy and will be a fine man.'

'Who will always be welcome in our home,' she finished.

'He is alone now. He needs my…' He paused. 'He needs our help.'

She nodded. 'And we both know how hard it can be to lose a parent.' Then she frowned. 'I have but one question left.' She poked him sharply in the ribs. 'Who is Mary and why is she taking my place as my sister's friend?'

'Mary?' He laughed.

'Mary,' she repeated, not bothering to contain her jealousy of the interloper.

'Mrs Mary Lovell,' he replied.

'Your…?'

'Aunt,' he finished. 'Let us say, for convenience's sake, that she is my aunt. As long as there are people who believe the story about my father the Duke, I would not want my mother to be the subject of speculation. As Belle's caregiver, she will be living a scant mile from my home.'

'Where you can see her whenever you like,' she said, smiling and snuggling back against his chest.

He nodded. 'It is time that I made amends. It will be good as well for Belle to have a new friend. And it will leave you free to marry. You would be living as near to your sister as I am to my mother.'

The arrangement was almost too perfect and she thanked him for it with a kiss that left them both breathless. When they parted, she asked, 'Is the scandal of your changing sisters greater or less than that of my sister's elopement?'

'At this point, there are so many secrets between us, I cannot rank them,' he said. 'I have already procured a special licence. But if you wish to rival your sister, my carriage stands waiting and we can set off for Scotland immediately.'

She thought for a moment, then ran a hand down his chest to press against his heart. 'I think the sooner the better. But choose what you wish. I have strict instructions to say yes to you, no matter what you request of me.'

He froze and she felt the beat against her hand increase. Then his hands on her back strayed lower, well past the bounds of propriety. 'Anything?'

'Anything,' as he pressed her body tight against him.

And now he was walking slowly forward, pushing her towards the sofa in the corner and down until the weight of his body had sunk hers deep into the cushions. 'Then, my dearest Amy, if you don't mind, I think I shall rephrase the question.'

* * * * *

If you enjoyed this story, you won't want to miss these other great reads from Christine Merrill:

THE GREATEST OF SINS
THE FALL OF A SAINT
THE TRUTH ABOUT LADY FELKIRK
A RING FROM A MARQUESS
THE SECRETS OF WISCOMBE CHASE